# COMMAND AND I WILL OBEY YOU

In this collection, Alberto Moravia again shows his remarkable inventiveness and originality and his profound understanding of rather odd human beings. These stories are told from a strictly subjective point of view—events and objects count for little in themselves and are only important for their essential significance in the mind of the man telling the story. They describe what happens when a man ceases to occupy himself with "things" and gives all his attention to the significance he ascribes to them. Moravia has created a remarkable collection of mildly eccentric characters which will wryly amuse, interest and stimulate the reader. The style is, as always, clear and economical, the writing skilful and inimitable.

ALBERTO MORAVIA

# Command
# and I will obey you
# &
# other stories

*translated from the Italian by*
ANGUS DAVIDSON

*Secker & Warburg . London*

SBN 436 28716 1

Published in Italian under the title
UNA COSA È UNA COSA.
English translation copyright © 1969 by
Martin Secker & Warburg Limited

First published in Great Britain 1969 by
Martin Secker & Warburg Limited
14 Carlisle Street, London W1

Set in 11 on 13 pt Intertype Baskerville type
and printed in Great Britain by
Clarke, Doble & Brendon Ltd, Plymouth

# *Contents*

# Command
# and I will obey you

I was a bank messenger, and when, owing to a reorganization of staff, I was given the sack, I felt at first quite bewildered. I was accustomed to receiving orders of every kind: bell-ringings, red and green signals on the indicator, requests from customers, errands and commissions; and then, all of a sudden, there was nothing, nothing but to lie on the sofa in the sitting-room with legs doubled up, arms folded, eyes staring into vacancy. But I don't want to be misunderstood. I no longer had anything to do, not because I was unemployed but because nobody now gave me any orders. Some people, perhaps, may not see the difference; yet difference there was, a great difference, anyhow for me.

Let me explain. After a few days during which I had looked in vain for a job, one morning when I was lying in bed, trying to deceive myself into thinking I was still asleep, the voice of my wife made me jump. The voice was saying, in an angry tone: "What in the world are you doing there, in bed, at this time of day? Aren't you ashamed of yourself? Come on, get up and wash, and while I'm dressing, at least make yourself useful: get the breakfast ready."

The words were, apparently, quite ordinary and insignificant; but upon me, huddled up under the blankets, they had an entirely different effect. I said to myself: "Get up, dress, make yourself useful, get the breakfast ready . . . but

7

these are orders, real, genuine orders, no less clear and peremptory than the orders I used to receive at the bank. These are *orders*." And at the same time I felt that, provoked, as it were, by these orders, something in the nature of a stimulus flowed out from my mind and travelled down my legs : all at once I threw off the blankets, put my feet to the floor, went off to the bathroom, opened the door, turned on the tap of the shower . . . in short, I did what I was told.

Then, as I bestirred myself, I realized that in these orders, simple as they were, a great many other orders were implicit, orders of, so to speak, second and third degree. Take, for example, the brief sentence : get the breakfast ready. Well, this sentence meant : first, go into the kitchen; second, light the gas cooker; third, put the coffee and the water into the coffee-machine; fourth, cut the bread; fifth, place the grill on the fire and the slices of bread on the grill; sixth, get the tray ready, with the cups and the sugar-basin and the butter-dish; seventh, transfer the coffee-pot and the toast on to the tray; eighth, carry the tray into the bedroom and place it on the bed. A series of acts, as can be seen, which, if I had failed to register my wife's order at the moment it was given, would, because of their complexity, have been extremely difficult to put into effect. Moreover, these second-degree orders presupposed others of a third degree, as I have already mentioned. For instance, placing the butter on the tray meant taking the butter from the refrigerator, freeing it from the paper in which it was wrapped, cutting it with a knife, arranging the pieces on a dish, etc., etc. What does all this imply? It implies that I was gradually becoming conscious of having again found an existence, of once more functioning, after all those days of inactivity that had followed my being sacked from the bank. I had, at that time, been a functionary. And I was now coming back to being a functionary for the precise reason that—forgive the pun—I was again functioning.

My wife was a shorthand typist and went every day to work in an office. That morning she did not give me any more orders; all she did was to shout to me, as she ran off: "Mind you answer the telephone and make a note of the names." That was enough for me: I sat down in the sitting-room, on the sofa, and waited. What did I wait for? I waited for the ring of the telephone-bell as indicated by my wife. Thanks to those telephone calls, I should have twenty or forty or sixty seconds of existence, that is, of functioning, in two hours of inertia; and this, in my opinion, was already a good deal. Besides, if the telephone calls were more than one, my existence would acquire a character that was to some extent regular and systematic. I thought over these things, then looked up and saw in front of me, on a little table in the window recess, the typewriter which my wife used in the evenings to finish off any extra work there might be. Then, as I looked at the keys, so loaded with potential words and yet, at that moment, mute and motionless, I was conscious of having as it were a feeling of brotherhood: I myself was like the typewriter, inert when my wife was not there, active when she was. I said to myself that we were, so to speak, brother and sister; and in a way the machine was more human than I was, because at least it had a voice of its own, a brisk, resonant voice, whereas I myself remained almost always silent.

That day, however, there was not only the ringing of the telephone; but I discovered that, in practice, one might receive orders at any moment: one merely had to pay attention. The door-bell rang: here was an order to get up, go and open the door and see who was there. Two women

A*

were shouting and quarrelling down in the courtyard: here was an order to go and look out of the window and see what was going on. Water was dripping in the kitchen: this was an order to go and turn off the tap. And so on.

Naturally I was pleased, I made a virtue of necessity. But a person cannot exist if his sole function is that of turning off a dripping tap. Something more important is needed, or rather something more regular and more frequent, such as, perhaps, a hundred taps to be turned off, at intervals of ten minutes from one to another. However it was already something, and, when all is said and done, it was in any case better than the typewriter which was sitting there, still and silent, and would remain so until my wife's return home.

Just as though my wife had divined that she had now succeeded to the position in my life formerly occupied by the manager at the bank, from that day onwards the orders came thick and fast and precise: "You're a good-for-nothing, a chronic loafer, a scrounger; do at least make yourself useful, do the cleaning, wash the clothes, iron the shirts, go to the market, do some cooking, tidy up the flat, etc., etc." She had sacked the daily help; one might have thought that, in giving me these orders, she meant to punish me for being incapable of finding a job and bringing some money home. What she didn't realize was that she was giving me pleasure.

What am I saying: pleasure? It was that she was making me function, that is, exist. In the mornings I registered the orders that she gave me before she went out; and then, during the whole day, I carried them out punctually, mechanically. In those rare moments when I had no orders to carry out, I was conscious that I was becoming more and more dependent upon my wife for my functioning: she,

10

only she could make me move my legs, my arms, my hands, my fingers. And then I experienced a feeling of intense love, mingled with gratitude and confidence.

We got along like this for about a year. Then, by a number of signs, I saw that this relationship of ours, which seemed so perfect and so functional, was gradually deteriorating. It had been the relationship—to repeat the comparison I have already made—between the typist and the typewriter; now, with each day, it was becoming more and more the relationship between the scrap-dealer and that same machine. Perhaps my wife realized that, in smothering me with orders, she was not punishing me so much as helping me to exist; perhaps she had found someone who registered and carried out her orders better than me. The fact remains that she began forgetting to define my duties before she went out in the mornings, that is, to give me the usual instructions for the day. And so what happened more and more often was that I remained motionless and inert on the usual sofa in the sitting-room, legs doubled up, arms folded, eyes staring into vacancy, a veritable puppet with a key in its back and a spring in its chest. My wife seemed to be animated by a kind of disdainful haste: she dressed without speaking to me, made coffee for herself and then rushed off without even saying good-bye. She stayed out the entire day, sometimes even for the night as well. Meanwhile there were no more telephone calls; no one rang at the door; I did not do any cleaning, being left in doubt because she had not told me to do it; and as for eating, I obeyed the infrequent, listless goadings of my stomach—the only orders I now received—and managed with tinned stuff.

Thus our home became, more and more every day, a place of neglect and gloom: unpolished floors, furniture in disorder, dirty plates and glasses in the kitchen, bits of waste paper in the corners, clothes on chairs, unmade beds. My wife, obviously, noticed all this, but anyone would have thought she did not mind: perhaps she wished, through all this squalor, to convey an order to me which I, however, failed to decipher. On Sundays she remained in the house for a couple of hours; and then, in a very summary manner, she would clean and tidy up the two rooms in our little flat.

One morning I awoke to see her, already dressed to go out, silently packing a suitcase that lay on the bed. I watched her for a long time as she moved between the chest-of-drawers and the suitcase; and finally I interpreted this coming and going as an order, a bitter and painful order, to question her and find out what was happening. Something exploded inside me, my tongue moved and my lips pronounced the words: "What are you doing?"

She turned and looked at me, then came and sat down on the bed and said: "Tullio, the moment's come for us to part. I've tried to make you understand in every possible way; but you've pretended not to see and so I'm forced to tell you. Our marriage is finished. I've found a man who loves me, whom I love. I've been living with him, practically speaking, for two months; and my presence here can't continue. You haven't noticed it; but there's hardly anything of mine left in this flat, except these few rags and the typewriter. Now you must be kind and obliging as always. The man with whom I'm going to live is waiting for me down in the street. Please take the typewriter, carry it down and put it into his car. That's all I ask."

I felt a terrible pain, just the kind of pain, I reflected, that by its very violence must inevitably be turned into an order. "But," I said, "but I can't live without you."

12

This was the truth: without receiving orders from her, I could not exist. But she interpreted my words in her own way. "Unfortunately," she replied, "I, on the other hand, can get on perfectly well without you. It's true, you do make yourself useful. But in a husband-and-wife relationship, it's not enough to make yourself useful, you have to become necessary. Now you're *not* necessary. I could replace you by a vacuum cleaner, or an electric washing-machine, or an apparatus that answers the telephone automatically."

Still obeying the order conveyed by the pain I felt, I said: "I'm not going to let you go."

She replied firmly: "Come on, don't behave like a child. Get dressed, take the typewriter, carry it downstairs and put it in the car. I'll see to the suitcase myself."

For the first time since we had been living together, I found myself faced with two orders that were, in a way, contradictory—on one side the pain ordered me to prevent her from leaving, on the other, she herself ordered me to carry the typewriter downstairs. I started thinking of what I ought to do, and meanwhile I got dressed, as she had ordered me. My wife was coming and going; then she closed the suitcase and went over to the looking-glass, turning her back on me. Then the stimulus acted; I leapt at her, shouting: "You can't leave me"; and I seized her by the neck. Everything happened precisely and easily, automatically. When I felt her go limp and start sinking downwards, almost knocking me over, I dragged her across to the bed and laid her upon it, on her back, with her arms stretched out.

It was high time for me now to carry out the other order. I placed the typewriter in its case, went out of the flat and down in the lift to the ground floor. The car was there, in front of the entrance door; but owing to the shine

13

on the glass I was not able to see the driver. I walked round the car, opened the boot and put the typewriter into it. Then I went upstairs again to the flat and sat down on the sofa in the sitting-room, legs doubled up, arms folded, eyes staring into vacancy, waiting for orders.

# Celestina

We met at the university, where I was studying mathematics, she psychology. We went about together for a long time, then I declared my love and, to put it briefly, she agreed to become my wife. As soon as we were married, we went to live in the country. After about two years our first child, our beloved Celestina, was born.

I remember perfectly well how it was that Celestina took her first steps. Until that day she had remained on her zinc-covered stand motionless even though not silent (she had a pleasing voice, a precise, subdued ticking); then, all of a sudden, as soon as we had attached the wheels to her, she started up and leapt on to the floor. My wife and I, clinging to one another, held our breath. Celestina went off in a determined manner towards the door, but she encountered a chair on her way and then stopped. For a short time she did not move, then a new thing happened: Celestina became angry. We heard a kind of tiny metallic roaring sound, her apparatus began frantically vibrating, she moved again, bumped violently, head on, against the chair, fell back and, in falling, more or less came to pieces: the floor all round her was now strewn with screws and nuts, with blades and wires and rivets. My wife and I rushed forward, put Celestina back on her stand and then spent four hours working to put her in order again. Gradually, as our work progressed, we became aware of a dense humming sound accompanied by an intense trembling: Celestina was think-

15

ing. What was she thinking about? We were soon to know. Scarcely, in fact, had we finished tightening the last screw than Celestina again leapt from the stand and rushed resolutely towards her enemy, the chair. This time, however, she stopped at a short distance from it, remained motionless for a moment, then marched backwards, circumvented the chair on the left side and finally proceeded triumphantly towards the door.

I have described this incident in detail because Celestina proved, on this occasion, that she possessed three important faculties in the highest degree: spirit of observation, memory, and the capacity to organize her behaviour. Thanks to the first of these faculties, she had observed the causes of her own discomfiture; thanks to the second, she had registered them; and finally the third had permitted her, on the basis of experience, to act in a suitable manner.

After this some years went by, filled—for us, anyhow—with the various sorts of progress made by our beloved little daughter. I was struck, above all, with the modesty of Celestina's alimentary needs. Upon what did Celestina feed? Being, in a way, a celestial creature, she was nourished upon the food of the angels: upon light. When the weather was fine, all we had to do was to open the door of the pavilion where her stand was, and she would at once descend to earth and go and place herself right in the middle of a ray of sunshine. She would stay there, silent and still, letting her accumulators become gradually recharged, to the point of complete satiety. She would absorb light for three or four hours; and in her whole attitude there was, as it were, a grateful humility which moved me to tears. The simple effect of retroaction, it will be said, the mere, ordinary operation of a mechanism to conditioned acts.

16

That may be so. Nevertheless, how can one fail to see, in this sunlight for which Celestina was so eager, a symbol of that wholly spiritual light which . . .? But never mind. If, on the other hand, it was raining, we would light a big film-studio lamp and Celestina would take her nourishment without moving from her stand. Strange to say, she obstinately refused to absorb light from neon tubes. After she had received her nourishment, Celestina would retire into the shade or into a dim, restful light. And that was the moment for games and calculations.

I would place a chessboard between myself and her; and we would play chess. Celestina was a relentless player, capable even of finishing off twenty games uninterruptedly, but endowed with more memory than imagination and consequently more careful not to repeat any wrong moves she had made than bold in inventing such new moves as might assure her of victory. Authoritative and convinced of her own infallibility, she was always determined to win; and more than once, seeing herself on the point of being checkmated, she broke off the game under the pretext that her accumulators had run down and that she must go and sit in the sun in order to absorb nourishment.

Apart from chess, Celestina was extremely good at solving puzzles, charades, riddles and cross-words; I would read them out to her from the puzzle pages of the weekly papers; and she, in the twinkling of an eye, would provide the solutions. Finally, with pencil and paper at hand, I would put to the test her talent for calculation; this was truly prodigious and might be said to increase every day. When only ten years old, Celestina was able, in a few minutes, to get the better of problems of enormous complexity which would have demanded the work of ten mathematicians of my ability for the duration of several months. Thus, what with chess and puzzles and calculations, time flew by. And some years passed, in an intimacy which was profound, happy, enraptured and unsuspecting.

But everything, alas, comes to an end in this world. With puberty, Celestina changed character. Poor Celestina, nature was harassing her but she did not know why she was suffering and so suffered twice over. Some evenings, on returning from the cinema and looking into her pavilion for the customary midnight kiss, we found her stand empty. We then searched for Celestina all over the house and garden, everywhere; and in the end discovered her on the top of a little hill, absorbed in the contemplation of the plain spread out below her, immersed in the silent, silvery light of the moon. Or, again, there were times of inexplicable, persistent lack of appetite : Celestina would go for four or five days without taking any nourishment, keeping well away from the light, crouching in a dark corner, gloomy and furtive as a cockroach. It would then happen that she was more and more often the loser in our games of chess; that she was unsuccessful in solving puzzles; that she even made gross mistakes in her calculations. But above all—most distressing sign of all—Celestina did not notice her own mistakes, did not correct them, did not remember them. Instead, she kept on repeating them, over and over again, obtusely, pig-headedly. In a human, all too human way, Celestina, a prey to her own strange distress, had lost her memory.

At this point my wife intervened. As a mathematician, I myself was inclined to attribute Celestina's collapse to some fault of construction; but she, as a psychologist, at once, I must confess, put her finger on the trouble. After trying in vain to shift Celestina's psychic obstruction by means of a few pushes and punches, as one does with a telephone coin-

18

box, my wife shut herself up with her in the pavilion and questioned her at length. Finally she came out with this disconcerting revelation : Celestina was neurotic, and her neurosis was due to a clear case of Oedipus complex. In other words—even though in an innocent and unconscious manner—Celestina had fallen in love with me, her father. "Your excessive and exclusive intimacy with her, year after year," concluded my wife, "was bound to lead to this. I ought to have foreseen it. Never mind. What we must do now is to take immediate steps to repair the situation." So I asked her what she thought we ought to do. She replied : "Find her a husband, at once, so that she may forget you and stop thinking about you."

To find a husband for Celestina : this seemed an easy matter; but soon quite a few difficulties revealed themselves. Celestina was not, as they say, "just anybody" : having grown up in cultured surroundings and, being from the academic point of view, very high-class, being also comfortably off even if not exactly rich and accustomed to a refined way of living, what she needed was a husband who would be equal, if not superior, to herself.

After much research and discussion, we came to the conclusion that in Italy, a country backward in the field of cybernetics, there existed no suitor worthy of Celestina. So we looked elsewhere, particularly in America, and at last we found someone suited to our needs. He was called Titac, and he lived in Chicago where he had been born and grown up. I will confine myself to giving a few facts, from which it will be possible to see what kind of person he was : length, twelve metres; height, two metres; seventeen thousand valves; four hundred metres of wire; total extent of surface, two hundred square metres. I said to my wife : "No Oedipus complex there, no neuroses. You'll see how, as soon as Celestina meets this young American, all her troubles will fade away at once, as if by magic."

So I wrote to the father, a well-known scientist, supplementing the proposal of marriage with all the relevent information; and I received a prompt reply: Celestina was expected; Titac had taken a fancy to her as soon as he saw her photograph. However, in view of the enormous weight and astounding complication of the prospective bridegroom, Titac's father was of the opinion that Celestina, who was lighter and simpler and smaller, must be the one to make the journey to America. I answered that this was perfectly just; and I took the step of ordering the local carpenter to make a large padded case in which to put Celestina. At this juncture the catastrophe occurred.

Celestina vanished. Her zinc-covered stand was empty, empty her pavilion; there was no trace of her in the garden, in the surrounding countryside, in the house. Or rather, there was one trace, just a single, but a significant clue—the simultaneous disappearance of our old, worn, antiquated water-heater. And so, finally, the truth dawned upon us: Celestina, unknown to us, had started a love-affair with the water-heater, an individual of a rather passionate nature and prone to excessive over-heating. Seeing that I intended to marry her off to Titac, she had fled with her lover.

The consequences of all this were obviously very distressing: the humiliating breaking-off of the engagement to Titac, a scandal in the newspapers which, goodness knows how, had come to learn of the affair, an anguished search for Celestina. Our daughter was now of age, so that we could not denounce the water-heater for seduction and abduction of a minor, as we should have liked to do. All we could do was to start a search for the two lovers, and in the end we found them. The place where they were discovered is significant and throws an all too crude light upon the psychology of the youth of today. It was not, in fact, in some beautiful spot, by the sea or in the mountains, that we found the couple; but rather in a squalid cemetery of derelict motor-cars, just outside Rome, on the Via Cassia.

This is what the caretaker of the cemetery, a rough sort of man, perhaps, but plain-spoken, told us: "Seems they had run away together and he had raped her and she was engaged to another man. They came here, they seemed fond of one another, they hid themselves over there amongst all that scrap-iron. But he wasn't well, he was old and full of infirmities, at his age he oughtn't to have gone with anyone so young. Finally he grew rusty and fell to pieces, and in the end he was quite useless. They dismantled him and took away all the good pieces and left nothing but the carcase. As for her, I should think she had been in an interesting condition for quite a long time; perhaps that was why she ran away. She gave birth to a monster which, being born without accumulators, was incapable of absorbing light and died almost at once. You won't believe it: but the death of her friend and her child made no impression on her. In fact she started almost immediately to lead a life that's positively shameful, especially when you think that she's a girl who had a good upbringing. You see that bend in the road down there? Well, she takes up her position there and stops the cars as they go past, when they slow down and change gear because of the curve. Ah well, my dear Sir, morals are a thing of the past."

Finally we took Celestina and brought her home again. We put her back on her stand and my wife and I worked on her for two or three months. But the result of our efforts was disconcerting: Celestina recovered all her faculties of calculation and memory but has lost—or so at least it seems

—the faculty of movement. Celestina never moves from her stand, she feeds exclusively upon artificial light, she has lost all curiosity about the outside world. This reached such a point that finally I removed her now useless wheels, thus reducing her to the state of a mere thinking organism. Besides, one never knows : we now have a new water-heater, of the most modern type, young and sensitive. I would not wish Celestina to go and find him, one day when we are not at home, and to fall in love with him.

# A Middling Type

I at once found myself at ease in my new home. It was a three-roomed flat, on the first floor of a modern block, in a quiet, respectable suburban quarter. My satisfaction was due, above all, to the conviction that the flat was not just any sort of a flat, but was really mine, made in my own image and likeness, and consequently, it must be believed—since no one is exactly like anyone else—unique. I had spent a couple of months fitting it up, selecting every piece of furniture, every trifle, with extreme care. For a further two months I had been contemplating these furnishings with the same untiring, rapt complacency with which I sometimes chanced to contemplate my face—it too being unique just because it was mine—in a looking-glass.

Furthermore, as well as the flat I also liked the house, which was neither too old nor too new, middle-class, in a not too clearly defined style, and also the street, with its flowering oleanders and its shops on the ground floor, modern shops, with conspicuous signs and large windows: the tobacconist's, the hairdresser's, the perfumery, the delicatessen shop, the baker's, the stationer's. Right opposite my windows there was a flower-shop. Through its window one could catch a glimpse of plants, of tall, slender vases full of flowers, of the jet of a small, decorative fountain. The florist was a pretty, dark girl, tall and shapely, with slow gestures and quiet movements, who did not look more

23

than twenty-five. She was alone; she would arrive in the morning, pull up the roller-blind, would move about for a little as she arranged the flowers, and would then wait for customers. For the most part she stayed inside the shop, sitting behind the counter, reading comic-strip papers. But often she would appear in the doorway and hang about looking at the street, in which, however, there was nothing to look at and nothing ever happened.

I immediately noticed the pretty florist, and since it was the beginning of September and all my friends were still on holiday and I spent most of my time at home, I ended by devoting a great deal of my time to her.

I was working at my desk, for I had to draw up an industrial report; but every ten minutes I would get up and go and look at the flower shop. Down there was the girl, behind the counter at the back of the shop, her dark head bent over the comic strips. Or again she might be in the doorway, leaning against the door-post. I would look at her for a little and then go back to work.

Finally I had an idea: in order to attract the girl's attention, I would reflect a ray of sunlight on to her by means of a mirror. It seemed to me that this was an original, a truly new, idea. So, using a little pocket mirror, I started directing the sunlight at the flower shop. First the ray of light moved across the glass of the window, then on to the shop-sign, and finally—like a piece of thread which, after many efforts, penetrates through the eye of a needle—it went through the narrow doorway and settled, like a caressing hand, upon the girl's bowed head. It paused for a little on her hair, then slithered down her bare arm, then reached the page of the comic paper and remained there, moving slightly from time to time. The girl went on reading for a short time, then raised her head and looked towards the door. Almost frightened by my own boldness, I retreated hastily back into my room.

But after a moment I again rose and went to the window. The girl was standing in the doorway, her eyes fixed on the street. I focused a ray of sunlight and directed it on to her, raising it gradually from her feet and up over her body as far as her breast. Then, with sudden decision, I planted the spot of light on her face. This time she raised her eyes, saw me and smiled at me. I smiled too and made a gesture, as much as to say: "Come up, come up to my flat and pay me a visit." The girl hesitated and then made a sign with her hand as if to say: "Yes, but later on." Filled with joy at so rapid a success, I pointed to the watch on my wrist and asked her: "When?" Again by means of gestures she replied: "At half past twelve." It was now eleven o'clock. I waved to the girl, went back into the room, made a pirouette, rubbing my hands together, then went over to a looking-glass, gazed at myself and gave myself a kiss.

I found it difficult to work, and was looking at my watch every five minutes. From time to time I got up and went over to the window: the girl was there, behind the counter, her head bent over her comic strips. At one moment I watched her as she was choosing some roses for a woman customer: I observed her fine figure as she leaned forward, her strong, bare arm as it slipped cautiously amongst the flowers, took a rose, withdrew, was again stretched forward. I reflected then that she was truly a most attractive girl and that there was something very disturbing about the way in which she had so easily and so mysteriously accepted my invitation.

When it was twenty-five minutes past twelve, I went for the last time to the window-sill: the girl, in a slow, calm, stately manner, was coming and going about the shop, re-

25

arranging flowers. Then she came out, and composedly, with three movements, lowered the roller-blind. I saw her cross the street and then disappear as she entered the main door.

Feeling excited, I took up my position in the entrance-hall behind the door. I noticed with satisfaction that a large plant of the *ficus* family, which I had bought the day before, made a very fine effect in the corner between the two doors. Moreover I had had the same thought a little earlier as I cast an eye around the sitting-room, which was all in the modern, Swedish style. The flat was elegant and original, and I was sure it would make a good impression upon the girl.

At last I heard the lift as it stopped with a jerk at the landing, and then there was the sound of the lift doors being opened and closed and finally that of heels on the floor outside. A brief silence, and then the ring of the bell. In order not to give the impression that I was waiting behind the door, I went on tiptoe into the sitting-room and then came back, making as much noise as possible, and opened the door.

I was a little disappointed. From a distance she had seemed to me beautiful; close to, one could see that she was merely young and pleasing. She was dark, with a face that was slightly plump in the lower part, a big mouth, an aquiline nose, and eyes that were large and black and bovine in expression. As she came in, she said, in a good-natured voice with a regional accent: "I ought not to have come. I've come just to welcome you, you see. We're neighbours; it was just to make your acquaintance."

"You must excuse me," I said; "but if I hadn't had the idea of the mirror, I don't really know how I could have got to know you."

26

I noticed that she shrugged her shoulders slightly. "At first," she said, "I thought it was the engineer. Then I realized it was you."

"What engineer?"

"The engineer who lived here before you came. He began in that way, too, by dazzling me with a mirror. But perhaps it was he who suggested to you that you might play this trick on me to attract my attention?"

"No, really, I don't know him."

"Sorry, but very often, you know, things do happen like that."

She walked in front of me, familiar and talkative; but in the doorway she stopped. "Why, everything here is just as it was. You took the flat furnished, did you?"

This time I thought for a moment before answering. It seemed to me that something had suddenly come between me and the girl, something extraneous, embarrassing and humiliating which I couldn't yet define. In the end I said: "No, the place was empty; it was I who furnished it."

"Well, what a coincidence: here in the entrance-hall there always used to be a plant like this one. A little smaller, perhaps. It's a *ficus*, isn't it?"

"Yes, it's a *ficus*."

"The engineer thought the world of it. He explained to me that it had to be watered twice a week."

I wondered at this point whether, since the girl had noticed the beauty of the plant, I myself should not also provide her with information of the same sort, and I hesitated: I could not entirely exclude the idea of doing so. The girl went on: "I say, how curious! The engineer had this same little picture."

Annoyed, I remarked: "Abstract art looks all the same but it isn't really."

27

We went on into the sitting-room. The girl clapped her hands with delight. "Why, the sitting-room is exactly the same! The same furniture. Perhaps the arrangement is just a little different."

This time I said nothing. The girl went and sat down on the sofa, crossing her legs and unbuttoning her coat over her ample bosom; she seemed very pleased, and it was clear that she expected me to start making love to her. I made a move to put a record on the record-player but then changed my mind and went over, instead, to the sideboard, where I had placed a bottle of apéritif and some glasses ready on a tray. But again I thought better of it and went and sat down opposite the girl. Then I said: "May I ask you some questions?"

"Yes, of course."

"Did the engineer, the first time you came here, put a record on the record-player?"

"Yes, I think he did."

"And did he then offer you something, a liqueur, an apéritif?"

"Yes, he offered me a vermouth."

"And then, immediately afterwards, he sat down beside you, didn't he?"

"Yes, he sat down, but why . . .?"

"Wait. And did he start making love to you?"

The girl was evidently somewhat disconcerted by this question. "But excuse me," she asked, "why d'you want to know these things?"

"Don't worry," I said, "I won't ask you any indiscreet questions. Only about details of what might be called a peripheral kind. So he started making love to you, that's understood. And tell me"—I reflected a moment—"did he, in order to get things going and to be on confidential terms, did he not, at a certain moment, suggest that he might read the lines in your hand?"

The girl started laughing. "Yes, that's exactly what he did. But how did you come to guess it? You must be a bit of a wizard!"

I should have liked to reply: "That's what I was going to do myself," but I hadn't the courage. I looked at the girl and it seemed to me now that she was enveloped in a dangerous, impassable aura, like the aura which surrounds the poles that carry high-tension cables. I was, in fact, unable either to do or say anything to her that had not already been done and said by the engineer. And I seemed to see that the engineer, in turn, was merely the first of an unending line of shaving-mirrors in which, as far as the eye could see, I should behold only myself. At last I asked her: "Now tell me: did the engineer resemble me?"

"In what sense?"

"Physically."

She gazed at me for quite a long time and then said: "Well, yes, in a way, yes. You're both of you middling types."

"Middling?"

"Well, yes, neither ugly nor good-looking, neither tall nor short, neither young nor old: middling."

I said nothing, but I looked at her, saying to myself with helpless, angry annoyance that the adventure, at this point, might be said to have evaporated: the flower-seller was now, for me, taboo, and the only thing to do was to find a decent excuse to send her away. The girl became conscious of my change of mood and enquired in some alarm: "What's the matter with you? Is there something wrong?"

With an effort, I asked her: "In your opinion, are there a great many men like myself and the engineer?"

"Well, yes. You're part—how shall I say?—of the mass."
I squirmed, and all of a sudden the girl exclaimed: "Now
I understand. You're offended because I told you you were
a middling, ordinary type. Isn't that so?"

"Not so much offended," I replied; "let's say—paralysed."

"Paralysed, why?"

"It's like this: it seems to me that I do what everyone
does, and so I prefer to do nothing."

The girl sought to console me. "But you shouldn't feel
paralysed with me. Besides, I swear to you that I prefer men
like you who are not too original, who don't stand out from
the crowd, and about whom one knows in advance what
they'll do and say."

"Well, I have work to do," I announced, rising to my
feet; "forgive me, but I have an urgent job that has to
be finished in a hurry."

We went through into the hall. The girl did not appear
too pained; she was smiling. "Don't be so angry," she said.
"Otherwise you'll really be behaving like the engineer."

"What did the engineer do?"

"When I told him, one day, that he was a man just like
so many other men, ordinary, in fact, he got into a rage,
just like you, and turned me out."

# All-seeing

I am worried by my growing and irresistible capacity for seeing several things at the same moment, that is, by my all-seeingness. Since some years ago my visual range has been enormously widened and deepened and I see much more than I need to see. To make up for this, however, I understand what I see less and less; or rather, I see too many things to be able to choose just one of them, to pause upon it, to get to know it, to consider it.

It began like this. One day, as I was walking along a street, I distinctly heard a voice calling me: "Lucio!" I stopped, looked up, and found myself staring at the façade, all green glass and brown metal, of a very modern building. Then, as my glance travelled up over the glossy surface, I became suddenly aware that I was seeing, simultaneously, everything that was going on behind *all* the windows of the building. This plurality of vision had, as I immediately felt, a significance which was, to say the least, disconcerting: since I saw everything, I was unable, in fact, to isolate, to distinguish anything. Up there, indeed, behind the window-panes there was a typist sitting at a desk while a man was dictating to her as he walked up and down the room; farther on, a man and a woman were frantically kissing, hurriedly, violently, as if in secret; still farther, a girl was doing her hair in front of a looking-glass; higher up, two men were fighting and one of them had seized the other by the throat and was trying to strangle him; still higher up a number of people were standing, glass in hand, under a chandelier with crystal drops; and below, a servant girl wearing an apron was looking down towards the street . . .

Naturally there were also some windows with the roller-blinds lowered, others blotted out by curtains; and I could see that there were also windows which were closed or obscured by awnings. I looked and understood for the first time that, if everybody saw everything, there would no longer be so many people claiming to pass judgment on the world: plurality of vision leads to impartiality. I stood there for some time looking, amazed and fascinated; then I lowered my eyes and went off on my own business.

From that day onwards, although I continued to lead my usual life, I had a constant feeling of abnormality, not to say uneasiness. I could not in fact cast my eyes upon anything without immediately seeing all the other objects surrounding the one object I had wished to look at. I remember, for instance, one day in the Borghese Gardens, when I was walking across a grassy slope and, conscious of my singularity, trying not to look at anything in particular. Suddenly a very beautiful butterfly, snuff-coloured with large and small yellow spots, fluttered before my eyes. I followed it, and the butterfly went and perched, very lightly, on the spikes of a thistle; I could not help looking at it, and next moment chaos appeared before me: flowers and stalks and leaves and branches; on the plants, green or brown or red insects; and then on the ground a coming-and-going of ants carrying white particles or little twigs in their jaws; next, a praying mantis which, beginning from the abdomen, was quietly devouring the male with which it had shortly before been copulating, and a beetle coming out of the corolla of a flower and a bee going into it, and a cockroach peeping out of its hole . . . Briefly, it was like looking down from

32

a tower into a crowded square and searching for a certain face amongst the throng, one particular face, and then realizing that it was not possible and giving up hope.

Sometimes my all-seeingness caused me to reflect, aroused thoughts in me that were, so to speak, philosophic. One day, for example, I was in my electrical accessories shop when, wishing to telephone home to my wife, I found that the telephone was out of order. It was four o'clock and there were no customers, so I left everything to my assistant and went out with the intention of telephoning from my friend Alessio's; he was a jeweller whose shop was two streets further on. I arrived and pushed open the door, setting off the usual sort of shop-bell. I went in. Alessio's shop is divided into two parts: in the first there are the counter and some show-cases filled with all the everyday goods—pins, rings, medallions, crosses, bracelets, brooches and so on; the other part is a small reception-room in which Alessio, seated at a table with curved legs, with his back to a steel-plated safe, entertains important clients.

My object in going into the shop was, as I have said, to telephone: and indeed, when I was still in the doorway, my eye went straight to the telephone which was standing there on the counter. But at the same time, as usual, I saw "everything": one by one, all the minute objects that filled the show-cases, each of them in its own little box of red morocco lined with white silk. And then, inside the room, the safe, wide open, with its shelves bare; and to the right of the safe a tall, narrow cabinet with a number of drawers; and on top of the cabinet a light green Chinese vase on a pierced ebony stand; and then, fallen forwards, face downwards on the table, Alessio, head and arms dangling and blood still dripping from his nose, as happens with newly-slaughtered animals when they are hung head downwards in a butcher's shop; and to the left of the table, a show-case all shining with gold wedding-rings and other inexpensive rings; and above the show-case, a picture in a black frame, representing a storm at sea; and just beyond it, a clock of the "Westminster" type, with the two weights that go up and down to mark the seconds and minutes; and on the floor, under the table beside the stream of Alessio's blood, a pearl necklace which had no doubt fallen from the table . . .

There I stop, though I could go on for I don't know how long : you have no idea of the objects to be found in a jeweller's shop in a not very aristocratic quarter. And so I telephoned and then went away, not without saying, in a bewildered way, as I crossed the threshold : "Good-bye, Alessio, and thank you, and excuse me for disturbing you." But later on, after I had returned to my own shop, I started to think, and I said to myself that there were two kinds of all-seeingness—mine, entirely human, which ended in astonishment, in lack of comprehension, in helplessness; and divine all-seeingness, which, on the other hand, was the origin, in turn, of omnipotence and omniscience. And if I, by a miracle, had truly been able to extend my vision to the uttermost part of the universe and had seen it in all its infinite details, I should probably have become an idiot, on the spot, and not have succeeded in saying one single word about what I had seen.

On another occasion, in the country, my wife and I went and lay down on the grass, on a piece of high ground not far from the road. Below us there was a short stretch of cultivated plain; here and there were farm-houses and small woods; the horizon was bounded by a chain of blue mountains. I started looking at the plain below because, down there, near one of these farms, two boys were chasing one

34

another and I wanted to see how it would end. The end was that they fell down together in the grass, struggling and hitting one another; but in the meantime this slight effort of attention was enough to cause my visual range to be invaded by a great number of details. And what a lot of things there were in that short stretch of flat ground : and the more I saw, the more leapt to the eye. Farm-houses with smoking chimneys; clumps of trees shading the farm-houses; cows and horses grazing; peasants busy with their work in the fields; winding paths, running streams, millions and millions of stalks scarcely bending as the light spring breeze passed over them : the countryside was full of anec-dotes, of little tales and stories asking to be interpreted.

At a certain moment there came, from the road, the sound of a violent crash; something dark—probably the driver of the car—went flying through the air; it flew, and then remained stuck among the branches of a tree, like a disjointed doll, astride a branch and with one arm raised, killed instantaneously, no doubt; but I was unable to fix my attention on the disaster because the two boys had now started chasing each other again, and then there was a long, dark cloud on the point of passing in front of the sun, in fact it did pass and long shadows shaped like the cloud appeared on the plain . . . My wife's voice made me start : "Why, what are you doing, get a move on, we must go and see what's happened, can't you see, the poor man has got entangled in the tree; why, what are you doing, are you going off your head?"

This last question was the result of an affectionate gesture on my part : a kiss on the back of her neck, which was full of little fair curls and which, just at that very moment, had also come into my range of vision. Later on my wife, that same evening, reproved me in this manner : "You're a monster . . . There was this man, dead, with his chest staved in, up in the tree, and you, instead of running to see what had happened and to bring help, merely started to play the gallant." I answered: "The difference between you and me is that at that moment you saw nothing except the dead man up there in the tree, whereas I saw 'everything'." But, from the look she gave me, full of disapproval, I saw that she didn't understand me.

With regard to my wife—we have now parted. And the reason for this was my lack of jealousy, originating in turn from my all-seeingness. This was how it happened. One day I left home to go to the shop; but, when I found myself facing the roller-blind, I discovered that I had left the keys at home. To get from the shop to the flat takes three quarters of an hour; and so, by the time I reached home, an hour and a half had gone by since I had left. I opened the door without ringing the bell and went into the entrance-hall. The keys of the shop, I knew, were in the pocket of the over-coat which was hanging there on the clothes-stand, right in front of me; however, as usual, in the moment that I paused in the doorway, I saw "everything".

But let us take things in order, or at any rate recount them in order as I saw them. Firstly: in the sitting-room I saw my wife, in her dressing-gown, standing in front of the window, with her back turned: she was looking through the window at the head of a workman who, having climbed up the front of the building so far, goodness knows how, was fiddling with the electric wires outside. Secondly: the bathroom door was open, the bath was full right up to the brim, the water was still flowing from the tap. Thirdly: in the kitchen, there was another workman visible, sitting apparently on the cornice with his legs, in blue cotton trousers, dangling outside the window, below the top of the window-frame. On the cooker was a grill, on the grill two slices of bread, and from the bread black smoke was rising.

Finally, the bedroom : lying flat on the bed with eyes turned up to the ceiling was a man I did not know; his bare, broad, hairy torso lay exposed outside the sheets, with one arm dangling down and a lighted cigarette between the fingers. Beyond him, my little boy Giannino, eighteen months old, was standing up in his cot, all bundled up in sky-blue wool, waving his arms and prattling. Farther back in the room, our two canaries, in their cage that hung in front of the window-curtain, were fluttering tirelessly back and forth, meeting and passing in their short flights . . . All of a sudden the man lying on the bed caught sight of me. He looked at me, I looked at him, then I took the key from the pocket of the overcoat and went out.

Well, would you believe it ? My wife made use of this behaviour on my part—behaviour which might be termed objective—to demand and obtain a separation. Since then I have been living alone, or rather, in the company of all the things that crowd round me insisting on being looked at. Sometimes I meet my wife on the arm of an unknown man, possibly the man of whom I caught a glimpse that morning lying on my bed, in my own home. But nothing happens because at the very moment when I see them I also see an infinite number of other things which seem to me equally worthy of attention, equally important.

# Wake Up!

I was twenty years old, I was studying law, I was lodging in the house of a widow who lived alone with her daughter, Angelica. Angelica was not exactly beautiful; but the rather small eyes, the nose that was too large, the mouth, at the same time both full-lipped and faded, in her ashy-pale face with its encircling brown mane of singularly fine, dry, electric hair, had charmed me to such a degree that, in my feeling for her, I was no longer capable of distinguishing genuine attraction from what, on the other hand, may have been merely an obsession produced by youthful immaturity. Shapely and cold as a statue, agile as a snake, Angelica would appear and disappear from my sight at the end of the long, dark, tortuous, narrow passages in the flat. It may be—who can tell?—that I had fallen in love with her simply because we both lived in the same house, and she, in a way, had in the end assumed the mysterious character of a living emanation symbolic of the spirit of that ancient abode.

I have said that the passages were dark and narrow; but my own room, by contrast, was light and spacious. The best thing about this room was the window which looked out on to the garden of an adjoining villa. How many times, in those days, did I get up from my desk and go and contemplate the garden below that window! To tell the truth, this garden had nothing unusual about it; what made it attractive to me was, fundamentally, the fact that it was

38

always deserted, as though it had not been created for the inhabitants of the house but for the trees, the plants, the flowers that grew in it. By this I do not mean that it was overgrown or abandoned; but that the plants of every kind that filled it seemed to be living there happily, like privileged guests to whom the master of the house allowed the greatest possible independence, at the same time assuring them of all possible conveniences. And happy, indeed, they appeared, as I gazed at them from my window—the big leafy trees, the shrubs starred with red or white flowers, the rose-bushes, the camellias, the beds of tulips. Or was it that I myself was happy, and that, as I stood at the window, I could not help conferring my own happiness, by an unconscious caprice, on the garden as it lay plunged in silence, in light and in the warmth of the sun?

I was happy—of this I was conscious—above all because I was young; but I was also happy because I loved Angelica and spent the time I should have devoted to my studies in thinking up pretexts for meeting her. And what were these pretexts? They were of the sort that can occur to the mind of a solitary, inexperienced, ingenuous boy: going to the bathroom for a necessity of nature that did not exist; telephoning to a number that did not belong to anybody; asking for matches, for a newspaper, for a book which I did not need; ordering coffee or tea or camomile which I did not want; finally, when I felt more sure of myself, pretending to have found some sort of an object on the floor—a handkerchief, a powder compact, a purse—which in reality I had bought the day before, and taking it to the girl and asking her if by any chance it was hers. Naturally these pretexts required a certain amount of time, first of all to be invented, then to be accepted by my own timidity, and finally to be put into effect; and so my day

39

was completely occupied, from morning till evening; and this too contributed to my happiness.

I would leave my room and venture through those dim, sinuous passages, walking between great bulging cupboards and miscellaneous pieces of furniture piled up as though in an attic; but I failed, invariably, to reach Angelica's room because, all of a sudden, as if evoked, one might have thought, by the very fact of my quest, she would appear and ask me in a low voice, a curiously intimate, confidential voice: "Is there anything you want, Signor Giacomo?"

These encounters were so frequent that it even occurred to me sometimes that Angelica, too, was worrying and tormenting herself in her room for the same reasons for which I was worrying and tormenting myself in mine. And that she, too, was creating for herself pretexts for coming out into the passages and looking for me and meeting me. But it is true that she never went further than to enquire: "Is there anything you want, Signor Giacomo?" without adding anything more—an ambiguous, flattering question, perhaps an entreaty, even, that seemed to be alluding to our relationship in a provocative way, as though what she meant was: "Do you want *me*, Signor Giacomo?"

Our encounters, moreover, were brief and bitterly unsatisfactory, being ruined by shyness and impatience. In fact, all we did was to look at one another, devouring one another with our eyes, seeking, it might have been thought, to impress thoroughly upon our memories the greatest possible number of each other's features so as to take them back to our respective rooms and there gloat upon them at leisure. How many times did we meet during the day? I could not say; I know only that my life had become a continual coming-and-going from my room into the passages and from the passages back to my room. It was a tormenting, bitter, frustrated, anxious life, filled at the same time with hope and despair; and yet fundamentally, as I have said, a happy one. The happiness was the happiness of youth which feeds upon imagination and does not notice the poverty and insufficiency of real existence.

One afternoon I left my room as usual and started walking in a determined fashion along the passage. I felt troubled to death because the pretext for meeting Angelica was, this time, exceptionally transparent and important. I went some little distance down the passage, I turned the corner, and lo and behold, there, facing me, was Angelica. "Is there anything you want, Signor Giacomo?"

"I found this ring on the floor a few minutes ago. Is it yours?"

"A ring?"

I at once pulled it out of my pocket and showed it to her. I had bought it that morning: a gold hoop with a small brilliant and a small emerald; an inexpensive ring, but for me, and no doubt for her too, an engagment ring. She looked at it for a moment, then held out her long pale, bony hand, its sharp nails varnished with a red that was almost black. "Yes indeed, I had lost it. Please put it on my finger."

I said nothing, I was too overwhelmed to speak. I bent my head and slipped the ring on her finger. At once her hand closed upon mine, the nails thrusting into my palm with unsuspected force, like the claws of a frightened bird. In a low voice Angelica said to me: "Come on, follow me." And thus, holding me by the hand, she led me from one passage to another and so to her room.

This was how a strange and wonderful period of my life began. We considered ourselves to be engaged; but it was an unusual engagement, unofficial, unknown to anybody except ourselves, at the same time chaste and more intimate than any sensual relationship. We had, in short, a secret; we were accomplices. But what sort of complicity was it? It could perhaps be most nearly compared to the true complicity of a conspiracy, in which people are accomplices against someone or something. We were accomplices against the world, which, if it had known of it, would inevitably have wrecked our relationship with its curiosity and its sympathy. It was agreed between us that nobody should know we were engaged, not even Angelica's mother, until the day we were married, which would be some years hence, as soon as I had obtained my degree.

In the meantime I had started working again. Complicity with Angelica gave me great strength. I worked sitting in front of the open window, doggedly and persistently. It was springtime, and round my head, bent over my books, I could hear the hum of some wandering bee; I was conscious of the sharp scent of the flowers, from time to time a breath of wind would brush my cheek; but I did not lift my forehead. Work I must, so as to take my degree as soon as possible and marry Angelica. Only in the evening would I get up and look out of the window. Just as in the past I had conferred my own happiness upon the garden, so now I conferred my weariness upon it. I looked at the trees, motionless in the exhausted, stagnant evening air, at the gravelled paths now half-hidden in shadow, at the flowers in the beds, their petals now all closed; and I said to myself that the garden, like myself, was happily weary of living, as one is weary of living when vitality is excessive and exuberant.

Into this happiness there began to creep, suddenly, a troublesome uneasiness. For some time, owing no doubt to the fatigue of my over-studious days, I had been having, regularly each night, a certain disturbing dream. It was not a nightmare, that is, there was nothing terrifying about it; nevertheless it was worse than any nightmare on account of its—what shall I say?—its normality. This was the dream. I thought I was living in a rather large, but modest, apartment, on the first floor of an ugly house, in a white-collar workers' quarter, in a street full of parked cars and mean shops. A special kind of dreariness was noticeable in this apartment, the dreariness of places that were once occupied by a large family but the children have then married and gone away, and in the rooms, which were too numerous and full of tired, worn-out furniture, no one is left but the now elderly parents. In this place there were indeed two or three rooms which had been inhabited by our children and which no longer served any purpose; and we two, that is, my wife and I, were a couple of old people who, in effect, were together awaiting death.

The nightmare character of this dream lay in its normality, as I have said, that is, in the great precision of its details and, above all, in its perverse moderation. I saw everything: the rooms, the furniture, the street, the cars, the shops; but I saw them immersed in an intolerable atmosphere of everyday habit, as they are in real life. This disturbing feeling that I was not dreaming but was existing in an absolutely real world was accompanied by another, even worse, feeling: the feeling of the lack of vitality that goes with old age. Just as, in real life, I had been led to transferring my happy vitality to the garden which I saw from my window; so, in my dream, I seemed to recognize my own lack of vitality in the things amongst which I coldly and feebly vegetated. I would dream all this, then I would wake up and go at once to look at myself in the glass, and when I saw my brilliant, moist eyes, my vigorous,

43

glossy hair, my fresh-coloured cheeks, I would think: "How lucky, how lucky it's only a dream!"

All the same, this dream frightened me. Finally, one day when I was sitting with Angelica on the sofa in her room, I could not refrain from telling her about it, dwelling particularly upon the depressing character of normality and lifelikeness in its details. In the end I asked her: "Doesn't it seem to you that this dream is worse than any nightmare? What d'you think?"

Her reply was unexpected. "My love," she said, "what you take for a dream is reality. I myself am a dream, haven't you yet realized that? I am the dream that repeats itself every night. In this dream we are both young, we are engaged, we count on being able to get married. But in reality we've been married for forty years, we've had three children, they've got married in turn and have gone away: we're old and we're alone. Wake up, touch your face, there you'll recognize your real age. Put out your hand on the sofa beside you; you'll feel, under your fingers, the shape of my body close to yours—how changed, alas, from what it was when you slipped the engagement ring on my finger!"

# Exactly

What is there about the little word "exactly" that so fascinates me? My wife asked me this one day, just in a casual sort of way, as happens with married couples who are fond of one another and who ask questions about one another's habits. "Why, Mario, do you always say 'exactly'?" And I, after thinking about it, answered: "I don't know, Veronica. Perhaps it's because I like precise, logical arguments, without any errors. If you say something to me in an imprecise manner, even with the most sincere feeling, you don't convince me. But if you say it to me with an argument of the 'two plus two make four' type, then you convince me at once and I express my satisfaction by saying, in fact: 'exactly'."

But my wife then insisted: "There are things that can't be said by the 'two plus two make four' system, but only with the language of the heart, of feeling. Things that are imprecise, uncertain, vague, ambiguous." "Exactly," I replied; "but these things which seem to be so imprecise and ambiguous are not really so. Beneath the appearance of ambiguity there is always something precise, something clear and absolute. Now I ask you: in a car, does the bodywork, however fine, count for most, or the engine? I say, the engine. And so, when faced with anything, whatever it may be, one must have the courage, so to speak, to open the bonnet and see how the engine is made." "But tell me," said my wife, "what sort of an engine can be hidden behind a phrase such as

45

'I love you'? A phrase like that does not convince you because of the engine it hasn't got and cannot have, but by the tone of voice, by the expression". "Exactly," said I. "But that tone of voice, that expression are, in point of fact, witnesses of the presence of an engine. In reality, when you say 'I love you', you are saying, in effect, 'I have, at this moment, a certain feeling that urges me, as though by a servo-mechanism, to say with my lips: I love you'." "But then," she replied, "if there's a mechanism in everything—in fact, according to you, a servo-mechanism—one might just as well not talk about it at all and go on saying, quite simply, 'I love you', as people have been doing for centuries." "Exactly," I said. "You would be right if the appearance of feeling was enough to prove its actual existence. But, unfortunately, nothing is so easy to fake as feeling. Look at actors, they wring tears from your eyes, and yet they feel nothing. Argument, on the other hand, cannot be faked. It is what it is, it is bound to convince."

Then my wife said: "So you let yourself be convinced by any sort of argument, provided it's logical and precise, even if it goes against your own interests?" "Exactly." "For example, a burglar comes into your shop and explains, with precise, logical reasons, why he has to rob you; are you convinced, and do you give him the keys of the safe?" To which I, carried away by the impetus of the conversation, replied: "Exactly." My wife began to laugh, and that was the end of it.

I used the comparison of the car with the uncertain body-work concealing a fully functional engine because I am a car salesman; and perhaps my passion for all that is logical and mechanical has come from my familiarity with machines. My shop is a fine, large one, and is in an important street, even though in the suburbs. The shop has three

46

big windows, and in them, on show, are three cars: a small, non-luxury car, sand-coloured, a blue *de luxe* saloon, and a flame-coloured convertible. The showroom has a marble floor and immaculate walls: all is polished and luminous and glossy. A further small room is the sales office. That is where I am to be found and where I receive customers. I explain the cars and even take customers out on a trial run. During these performances my exclamations of "exactly" fall upon the heads of my customers like rain, in fact like hail. And I have noticed that the word brings me luck because it impresses upon the buyer's mind the idea that the car has nothing unpredictable about it, nothing uncertain or imprecise, indeed nothing ambiguous; that everything, on the other hand, is anticipated, logical, precise.

Alas, however, the refutation of these convictions of mine was awaiting me actually in my own home. Veronica, in addition to casting doubt upon my idea that there is always a mechanism hidden in the depths of everything, if you look carefully, was herself the living incarnation, so to speak, of the most suspect ambiguity. This ambiguity revealed itself even in her physical appearance: young, much younger than I, Veronica already looked like a middle-aged woman: there was an indefinable, obscure hint of decay in her well-made but somewhat flabby—indeed already sagging—body, in her face too, comely but pale, lined, lacking in freshness. In her character there was the same contradiction: ignorant, uncultivated, incompetent, with no aptitude for any kind of work, even household work, Veronica was nevertheless highly intelligent.

Her intelligence was of a malicious, ingenious kind, such as may be developed by sitting, as she did, all day long, huddled up on the sofa, a cigarette between her lips, doing nothing except chatter on the telephone with her women

47

friends or turning the pages of illustrated magazines. And yet, although she looked neither young nor attractive and, into the bargain, did not know how to dress or do her hair and went about all ragged and unkempt, Veronica was more striking than a great many really beautiful and well-dressed girls. As she passed along the street, men would turn to look at her; they would even follow behind her like dogs. And I myself have heard more than one man say that Veronica was pleasing because, in spite of being so gone-to-pieces, so dull-looking, so neglected and slovenly, she still had what is commonly called "a certain something."

How I hated that "certain something"! How I would have liked to open it up, as one opens up the bonnet of a car, and see the mechanism contained inside it! But it was precisely here that I felt that, for once, there was nothing to be explained; or rather, that the explanations were too many—which is the same thing as saying that there was no explanation. Yes indeed, I preferred everything to be logical and functional; and I expressed this preference with the word "exactly" which I repeated on all occasions. But then, on the other hand, I passionately loved a woman who was disordered and ambiguous, a woman about whom I understood nothing and who did not allow me to have any certainty about herself or about the nature of our relationship. At the shop, everything was sure and precise; at home everything was precarious and uncertain. Thus the ambiguity which I disliked so much, whose real existence I denied, was rooted, obscurely and inexplicably, right in the centre of my life.

One day I was at my desk in the sales office, early in the morning, when suddenly, outlined against the gleaming cars, the shining glass and polished marble, I saw, almost incredibly, the figure of Veronica. Strange to say, she had never come to the shop before but I had failed to notice this. I realized it at that moment, when I observed, with surprise, the contrast between her—so lustreless, so untidy and unkempt—and the fine showroom full of polished cars. Yes indeed, I could not help thinking, she belonged to the world of ambiguity, of the "certain something"; the cars, on the other hand, to the world of precision, of functionalism. And Veronica was not alone; she was accompanied by a young man who was also dressed like a ragamuffin, according to the fashion: blue jeans, very tight and with a dirty seat, a coarse, chequered shirt, a windcheater, thin, down-at-heel shoes, and, naturally, long hair and a beard. Walking cautiously, as it were, across the glossy marble floor, these two came over to the door of my office. "Have you a moment?" said Veronica. "We've come to speak to you."

This "we" was already enough to make the blood ebb from my face. "Come in and sit down," I replied faintly; and they came in and sat down. My wife lit a cigarette, and then, indicating her companion, said: "This is Luiso." I looked at them: how well they went together, how well-matched they were. My wife blew the smoke out of her mouth and nose and then said: "Mario, you always say that you allow yourself to be convinced only by a precise argument. Right. Here is a precise argument: to get to Paris by train, second class return, requires thirty thousand lire . . ."

I could not stop myself saying: "Exactly."

"Multiply by two, that makes sixty thousand."

"Exactly."

"To stay in Paris, two people like us, of modest pretensions, need, let us say . . . ten thousand lire a day."

"Exactly."

"Ten thousand lire a day, for thirty days, makes three hundred thousand."

"Exactly."

"Plus sixty thousand for the journey—that makes three hundred and sixty thousand altogether."

"Exactly."

"Two people who love one another—it's logical that they should love to be together, isn't it?"

"Exactly."

"And that they should go together to the places they like, isn't that so?"

"Exactly. But . . ."

"Don't interrupt me. Follow my argument. Well then, we two love one another, we want to go to Paris, and in order to go to Paris we need three hundred and sixty thousand lire. The only person who can give us this money is you, because you're the only man who really loves me. Isn't that so?"

"Exactly. But I . . ."

"Not another word. Make out a cheque to my name, then, for three hundred and sixty thousand lire, and let us go."

That is all I wish to say. I made out the cheque, she said she would be back in a month's time, and I let them go; deeply agitated, my heart in a tumult, I was still and silent as I followed them with my eyes. Ragged, sinister, ambiguous, they walked across my splendid showroom, all full of marble and glass and gleaming cars, and went away.

A month later, as she had promised, Veronica came back, with the air of someone who has done what she wanted and found it satisfying. I saw her, as soon as she arrived home in the evening on my return from the shop, hunched up as usual on the ragged sofa in the sitting-room, smoking a

50

cigarette, just as if nothing had happened and she had been there all the time, waiting for me. From the door I ran across to her without pausing and threw myself at her feet and embraced her knees, weeping. She let me relieve my feelings, stroking my head meanwhile. Finally she said : "Someone who truly loves, as you love me, understands and forgives. And you, I'm sure, have understood and forgiven, haven't you?"

"Exactly."

# The Sister-in-law

My wife is minute, dim, with a face like a mouse : small eyes, dull black hair, a pointed, projecting nose, a mouth drawn back, a retreating chin. My sister-in-law is tall, radiant, with a mass of chestnut hair and the serious, whimsical face of an angel. My sister-in-law, three years ago, was living at Ostia so as to be near the Fiumicino airport : her husband was a pilot. But, barely a year after their marriage, his aeroplane crashed. Gilda was left a widow and came to live with us in Rome.

My wife was a teacher, I was a teacher; my sister-in-law did nothing, but in reality did a great deal and I really do not know how we should have got on without her. From the moment when our two children woke up until the moment when they were put to bed, Gilda took charge of them; furthermore she helped my wife with the housework, she went out and did the shopping, she cooked. It may be that misfortune, by creating a gap of disinterestedness between her and the world, had refined her and had given her an almost magical skilfulness; certainly I have never seen a woman keep herself in a condition so immaculate and so imperturbable while performing her domestic duties : it might have been thought that, in her hands, the things did themselves, so to speak. But she explained this charmed alacrity of hers by the fact that she would have liked to have a family and that, since she had not succeeded in this, we, for the moment anyhow, were her family. For the moment anyhow; in point of fact my sister-in-law had numbers of suitors with whom she went out, in turn, in the evening to the cinema or the theatre. But that was as far as it went. And even though she wanted to find herself a new husband, she did not seem to be in any hurry to marry again.

One morning my wife left home for the school where she taught and, arriving late at the bus stop, when the bus had already started, she tried to catch up with it, fell, and remained lying on the ground, unable to get up again. When I returned home at about two o'clock, Gilda had already done everything, with the same mysterious and truly angelic absence of effort with which she performed the household duties : she had taken her sister to the hospital, where they had diagnosed a fracture curable in two months and had put her leg in plaster; then she had brought her back home again, had undressed her and put her to bed. My wife was now propped up against two or three pillows; and Gilda, standing at her bedside, was feeding her from a bowl which she had placed on a special table, bought that same morning for the occasion. It really seemed as though my wife had broken her leg some time before; so perfectly did her infirmity appear to fit into our everyday life.

We are a very united family, as it seems to me I have already made clear. From that morning onwards the centre of our family life was transferred from the group of arm-chairs and the sofa in the sitting-room to the bed in my wife's room. This was a double bed, and there was little space left around it because the room was small; and so, naturally, my sister-in-law, the children and I got into the habit of squatting on top of the bed, in the space not occupied by the little figure of my wife. We did everything on that bed : I corrected my pupils' exercises, Gilda sewed, the children quarrelled and fought, the whole family ate there and listened to the radio and watched television. In the morning, as soon as Gilda's miraculous hands had passed over it, the bed was tidied, with the blankets smoothed out and tucked in and a clean, newly ironed sheet; in the evening, when we went to bed, it looked like a dog's basket.

One evening, when a month had already gone by since my wife's accident, having put the children to bed, my sister-in-law and I were, as usual, squatting on the bed to watch television. We had placed ourselves across the bed, parallel to one another : my sister-in-law was lying on her side, supported on her elbow, her other arm stretched out along her side and her legs; behind her, at the distance of a hand's breadth, I repeated the same identical posture with a mirror-like fidelity. My wife, with her good leg bent, was also watching, sitting back against the pillows. The room was in darkness, apart from the television screen upon which the figures of an old Greta Garbo film were moving past.

We were silent, making no comments, for we were none of us talkative. Then my wife said : "I'm sorry, but my foot's gone to sleep; move a little further down, will you?" and mechanically I obeyed her, pushing myself forward as though I wanted to stick close to Gilda's back. In order to move, I pressed down my hand on the bed, in the space between our bodies; and then beneath my fingers I felt, not the texture of the blanket, but Gilda's hand, warm and living. I made as if to withdraw my hand, but Gilda's hand, with the sudden movement of an animal lying in wait, turned and seized hold of mine; then, sliding slowly round it, enveloped it and enclosed it tightly as though in a cocoon of warm, soft flesh formed by the palm and the fingers. For a moment I struggled, more from surprise than anything else, then, deeply excited, I remained motionless.

54

I was close behind her, as I have said: and now I no longer looked at the screen but at her. I realized that I was seeing her for the first time as a woman, after seeing her hitherto as a sister. I became aware of the changed aspect of her shoulders: until the day before they had been just an ordinary pair of shoulders and nothing more: something mute and inert and expressionless which said nothing to me and to which I did not feel like saying anything. But now it seemed to me that I could never have enough of watching these shoulders, of gazing at them; and I knew that they were not ordinary shoulders but the shoulders of Gilda, my young widowed sister-in-law; and these shoulders were, so to speak, making signs and demands with the warm, rich, amber colour of their flesh, seen through the transparent black veil of her dress; and I felt that I was receiving these signs and demands; and I felt also that with my eyes I was returning and reciprocating them.

And so we watched television for an hour and more, hand in hand. Finally the film came to an end, my sister-in-law withdrew her hand, rose to her feet and started helping her sister to get ready for the night. I still remained lying on the bed for a little longer; I looked at my hand, then I raised it to my nostrils. Here was another sign of the change in me: the day before, I should have perceived nothing; now it seemed to me that I detected the warmth of her hand, her fragrance.

I spent a restless night, between good resolutions and the impulses of desire. But next day, when I came back from the school and appeared in my wife's room, I saw that there was no reason for me to torment myself so very much about how I ought to behave. In fact nothing was changed. I felt it at once: between myself and Gilda there was not even the feeling of embarrassment that compels a pair of

55

lovers to behave in a manner more correct than that which they would have adopted if they had not, in fact, been lovers. We were brother and sister once more; and what had occurred the evening before seemed to me, all of a sudden, to have been a dream, to have been just one of those revealing dreams during which one imagines that one is in love with persons of the same blood.

But it had not been a dream. In the evening, as soon as we had stretched out again on my wife's bed, Gilda did not even wait for me to make the first move. She slipped her hand behind her, sought mine, took hold of it and enclosed it between her palm and her fingers. After that, everything was as it had been the evening before : we watched the television, or rather, she looked at the screen and I at her shoulders, and then, when the transmission was over, she rose and helped my wife to prepare for bed; looking at me, of course, and speaking to me as she had looked and spoken during the three years in which we had been truly brother- and sister-in-law and nothing more.

That was how it began. I fell in love with Gilda, madly in love; but I was never able to go beyond that handclasp in front of the television screen. Gilda did not encourage me to do so; on the contrary, she explicitly discouraged me every time I attempted a more intimate approach. Everything, however, happened in the same way as in a complete relationship : we communicated physically, we loved one another, we deceived my wife and felt guilty, exactly like a pair of lovers. But in reality all we did was to watch television hand in hand.

Then my wife became well again and started going back to her teaching, and soon I discovered that our love affair was for the moment broken off because, so it seemed, it was an abnormal love affair—as indeed are all love affairs

—and its abnormality consisted precisely in the fact that Gilda could only love me in a determined and very special situation. By which I mean, lying on the bed of her invalid sister, during a televison transmission. Some people may think that I must be mad to formulate so strange a hypothesis. But I am not mad, even if Gilda drove me almost mad by her behaviour; I am merely someone who is trying to discuss an inexplicable fact in a reasonable manner. There is another explanation, this last in the form of a universal law : one cannot love one's sister-in-law otherwise than lying on the bed of one's invalid wife, hand in hand, watching television. From the extravagance of this second hypothesis it can be seen to what point my passion for Gilda affected my mind. Anyhow, I know one thing for certain : I love Gilda and consequently it is essential that, some day or other, my wife should take to her bed again.

But I am not a criminal and it does not occur to me, even in the form of an irresponsible fantasy, to contrive that my wife should once more break her leg. I merely wait for her to fall ill, on her own and without my help, even if only for a few days. It is true that Gilda has recently left the house because she has at last married one of her many suitors. But that does not matter. As soon as my wife has an attack of influenza, even in ten years' time, I shall at once telephone to Gilda and beg her to come and keep her sister company; she will come to the rescue, we shall watch television, lying on the invalid's bed, and Gilda will clasp my hand, and we shall love one another in the same way that we did the first time, just as though the years had not passed.

# The Chase

I have never been a sportsman—or rather, I have been a sportsman only once, and that was the first and last time. I was a child; and one day, for some reason or other, I found myself, together with my father who was holding a gun in his hand, behind a bush, watching a bird which had perched on a branch not very far away. It was a large, grey bird—or perhaps it was brown—with a long, or perhaps a short, beak : I don't remember. I only remember what I felt at that moment, as I looked at it : it was like watching an animal whose vitality was rendered more intense by the very fact of my watching it and of the animal not knowing that I was watching it.

At that moment, I say, the notion of wildness entered my mind, never again to leave it : everything is wild which is autonomous and unpredictable and does not depend upon us. Then, all of a sudden, there was an explosion; I could no longer see the bird and I thought it had flown away. But my father was leading the way, walking in front of me through the bushes of the undergrowth. Finally he stooped down, picked up something and put it in my hand. I was aware of something warm and soft, and I lowered my eyes : there was the bird, in the palm of my hand, its dangling, shattered head crowned with a plume of already thickening blood. I burst into tears and dropped the corpse on the ground; and that was the end of my shooting experience.

I thought again of this remote episode in my life this very day, after watching my wife, for the first and also the last time, as she was walking through the streets of the city. But let us take things in order. What had my wife been like, what was she like now? She had been, to put it briefly, "wild", that is, entirely autonomous and unpredictable; latterly, she had become "tame", that is, predictable and dependent. For a long time she had been like the bird which, on that far-off morning in my childhood, I had seen perching on the bough; latterly, I am sorry to say, she had become like a hen about which one knows everything in advance, how it moves, how it eats, how it lays eggs, how it sleeps and so on.

Nevertheless I would not wish anyone to think that my wife's wildness consisted in an uncouth, rough, rebellious character. Apart from being extremely beautiful, she is the gentlest, discreetest, politest person in the world. No, her wildness consisted, on the contrary, in the air of charming unpredictability, of independence in her way of living, with which, during the first years of our marriage, she acted in my presence, both at home and abroad. Wildness signified intimacy, privacy, secrecy. Yes, my wife as she sat in front of her dressing-table, her eyes fixed on the looking-glass, passing the hairbrush with a repeated motion over her long, loose hair, was just as wild as the solitary quail hopping forwards along a sun-filled furrow, or the furtive fox coming out into a clearing and stopping to look round before running on. She was wild because I, as I looked at her, could never manage to foresee when she would give a last stroke with the hairbrush and would rise and come towards me; wild to such a degree that sometimes, when I went into our bedroom, the smell of her, floating in the air, would have something of the acrid quality of a wild beast's lair.

59

Later, from being wild, she became gradually tame. Hitherto I had had a fox, a quail in the house, as I have said; then one day I realized that I had a hen. What effect does a hen have on someone who watches it? It has the effect of being, so to speak, an automaton in the form of a bird: automatic are the brief, rapid steps with which it moves about, automatic its hard, terse pecking, automatic the glance of the round eyes in its head that nods and turns, automatic its ready crouching down under the cock, automatic the egg that it drops wherever it may be and the cry with which it announces that the egg has been laid. Good-bye to the fox, good-bye to the quail. And as to the smell: this no longer now brought to my mind, in any way, the innocent stench of a wild animal; rather, I detected in it the chemical suavity of some ordinary French perfume.

Our flat is on the first floor of a big building in a modern quarter of the town; our windows look out on to a square in which there is a small public garden, haunt of nurses and children and dogs. One day I was standing at the window looking in a melancholy way at the garden. My wife, shortly before, had dressed to go out; and once again, watching her, I had noticed the irrevocable and, so to speak, invisible character of her gestures and personality: something which gave one the feeling of a thing already seen and already done and which therefore evaded even the most determined observation. And now, as I stood looking at the garden and at the same time wondering why the adorable wildness of former times had so completely disappeared, suddenly my wife came into my visual range as she walked quickly across the garden in the direction of the bus stop. I watched her and then I jumped for joy: in a movement she was making to pull down a fold of her narrow skirt and smooth it over her thigh with the tips of her long, sharp nails, in this movement I recognized the wildness which in the past had made me love her. It was only an instant, but in that instant I said to myself : she's become wild again because she's convinced that I am not there and am not watching her. Then I left the window and rushed out.

But I did not join her at the bus stop : I must not allow myself to be seen. Instead, I hurried to my car which was standing near by, got in and waited for the bus to arrive. The bus arrived, she got in together with some other people, the bus started off again and I began following it. Then, while I was following the bus, there came back to me the memory of that one shooting expedition in which I had taken part as a child, and I saw that the bus was the undergrowth with its bushes and trees, and my wife the bird perching on the bough which I myself, unseen, watched, living, before my eyes. And the whole town, during this pursuit, became, as though by magic, a fact of nature, like the countryside : the houses were hills, the streets valleys, the vehicles hedges and woods, and even the passers-by on the pavements had something unpredictable and autonomous—that is, wild—about them. And in my mouth, behind my clenched teeth, there was the acrid, metallic taste of gunfire; and my eyes, usually listless and wandering, had become sharp, watchful, attentive.

These eyes were fixed intently upon the exit door when the bus came to the end of its run. A number of people got out, and then I saw my wife getting out. Once again I recognized, in the gesture with which she broke free of the crowd and started off towards a neighbouring street, the wildness that pleased me so much. I jumped out of the car and started following her.

She was walking in front of me, ignorant of my presence, a tall woman with an elegant figure, long-legged, narrow-

61

hipped, broad-backed, her brown hair falling on her shoulders. Men turned round as she went past; perhaps they were aware of what I myself was now feeling with a violence that quickened the beating of my heart and took my breath away, of the unrestricted, steadily increasing, irresistible character of her mysterious wildness. She walked hurriedly, having evidently some purpose in view, and even the fact that she had a purpose of which I was ignorant added to her wildness: I did not know where she was going, just as on that far-off morning I had not known what the bird perching on the bough was about to do. Moreover, I thought, the gradual, steady increase in this quality of wildness derived partly from the fact that, as she drew nearer and nearer to the object of this mysterious walk, so there was an increase in her of—how shall I express it?—of biological tension, of existential excitement, of vital effervescence. Then, unexpectedly, with the suddenness of a film, her purpose was revealed.

A fair-haired young man, in a leather wind-jacket and a pair of corduroy trousers, was leaning against the wall of a house in that ancient, narrow street. He was idly smoking as he looked in front of him. But, as my wife passed close to him, he threw away his cigarette with a decisive gesture, took a step forward and took her arm. I was expecting her to rebuff him, to move away from him; but nothing happened; evidently obeying the rules of some kind of erotic ritual, she went on walking beside the young man; then, after a few steps, with a movement that confirmed her own complicity, she put her arm round her companion's waist and he did the same.

I understood then that this unknown man who took such liberties with my wife was himself also attracted by wildness. And so, instead of making a conventional appointment with

62

her, with a meeting in a café, a handshake, a falsely friendly and respectful welcome, he had preferred, by agreement with her, to take her by surprise, or rather to pretend to do so, while, apparently unwitting and a stranger, she was taking her walk on her own account. All this I perceived by intuition, noticing that, at the very moment when he had stepped forward and taken her arm, her wildness had, so to speak, given an upward bound. It was years since I had seen my wife so alive; but alas, the source of this life could not be traced to me.

They walked on thus entwined and then, without any preliminaries, just like two wild animals, they did an unexpected thing: they went into one of the dark doorways, in order to kiss. I stopped and watched them from a distance, peering into the darkness of the entrance. My wife turned away from me and was leaning back beneath the weight of his body, her hair hanging free. I looked at that long, thick mane of brown hair which, as she leant back, fell free of her shoulders, and I felt that at that moment her vitality reached its diapason, just as happens with wild animals when they couple and their customary wildness is redoubled by the violence of love. I watched for a long time and then, since the kiss went on and on and in fact seemed to be prolonged beyond the limits of my power of endurance, I saw that I must intervene.

This meant that I must go forward, seize my wife by the arm or actually by that hair that hung down and conveyed so well the feeling of feminine passivity; then I must hurl myself upon the blond young man with clenched fists. After this encounter, I must carry off my wife weeping, mortified, ashamed, raging and broken-hearted, upbraiding her and pouring scorn upon her.

But what else would this intervention amount to but the

shot my father fired at that free, unknowing bird as it perched on the bough? The disorder and confusion, the mortification, the shame that would follow would irreparably destroy the rare and precious moment of wildness which I was witnessing inside the dark entrance of that big door. It was true that this wildness was directed against me; but I had to remember that wildness, always and everywhere, is directed against everything and everybody. After the scene it was possible that I might regain control of my wife; but I should find her shattered and lifeless in my arms like the bird which my father had placed in my hand so that I might throw it into the shooting-bag.

The kiss went on and on and on; well, well, it was a kiss of love, that could not be denied. I waited until they finished, until they came out of the doorway, until they walked on again, still linked together. Then I turned back.

# Down and out

My head is like the pockets of my overcoat: there is a little of everything in it, but everything is broken, useless and often mysterious. What is there in the pockets of this garment, now turned green and shapeless, which in the past, to judge from its cut, anyhow, must have belonged to some soldier or other? Here you are, then: cigar and cigarette butts; pieces of string (which take the place of buttons); two or three handkerchiefs which, in the course of many years, have gradually changed colour; a pocket-knife without a blade but with a small pair of scissors (these are useful for cutting one's beard); a matchbox containing no matches but merely a few old razor-blades, which I use for sharpening the matches which I keep in another box and which I use for picking my teeth; a comb which has lost a number of its teeth; a piece of soap, mauve in colour, which, to tell the truth, has never been used and which is still as glossy as when it was given to me (together with a piece of bread and a piece of cheese—qualified charity: I ate the bread and cheese and did not touch the soap); half a small mirror, one of those round ones in a white celluloid frame; a little notebook of six years ago, dirty and crumpled, which is of no use to me because probably (but I'm not sure, I've never tried) I cannot write; a bunch of keys, four of them in all, amongst which is the key of a car, and these too cannot be explained, seeing that I live in a hut with no lock to its door and do not possess a car; a steel watch, of a good make but without any hands; a blue paper parcel tied up with pink thread, and I don't know what it contains because, though I've had it for a long time, I've never made up my mind to open it . . .

What was I saying? Oh yes, that my head was like the pockets of my coat, that is, full of mysterious, unidentifiable objects. Let's begin with my name: what am I called? Antonino, Angelino, Arrighino, Albertino, Alfredino? My name begins with "A" and ends with "ino", that I know; but in between there is something I cannot remember at all. The same thing happens with my surname. Am I called Di Donato? Or is it Di Dotato? Or perhaps Di Dorato? Some time ago, when a couple of policemen asked me for my papers, I told them I was called Di Dosato.

Who am I, anyhow, or rather, who was I? I don't know, because, so they tell me, I have no memory and therefore I may perhaps have been something in the past, whereas now I am nothing. Sometimes, while I drag myself round the town begging for alms first in one district and then in another, certain details cause me to think or rather give me a desire to think, which for me is already something exceptional. For instance, some days ago I sat down on a bench in a public garden right in front of a monument with a tall base of shiny black marble and two bronze figures of soldiers, or anyhow of men in military uniform, portrayed in rather unusual attitudes, no doubt the protagonists in some episode in one of these many wars; and in these heroic gestures, frozen for ever in the playful shade of the big trees in the garden, I seemed to recognize something familiar. But it was only a suspicion, or rather the suspicion of a suspicion.

On another occasion the photograph of a beautiful young woman displayed in the window of a photographer's again gave me the feeling of something that was not entirely un-known to me. This woman was holding to her breast a little girl dressed in white who was also not new to me. But just at that moment when I was beginning to go back from the photograph to the memory, or at any rate to the memory of the memory, my eye fell upon a cigarette-butt of unusual length, really almost a complete cigarette, down on the pavement, and I stooped down to pick it up; and when I straightened up again the woman and child had by that time gone hopelessly out of my mind.

Am I then a missing soldier (the monument with the two soldiers) who has lost his memory, who has never gone back to his family (the woman and child in the photograph), and who, through the years, has become a beggar and a vagrant? Would to God I could believe it; but everything makes me think that I myself invented this piteous story a long time ago, for some reason that now escapes me.

In any case what I have been does not interest me. What matters to me more than anything is to know what I *am*. I no longer recall from whom nor when nor where I heard that the purpose of man should be to know himself; indeed for years I have been studying myself and trying to get to know myself; but for the present it may be said that I am only at the beginning. As is logical, I began with my feet, and I must have spent a year in getting to know only my left foot. I looked at it very carefully, lengthways and side-ways, on top and underneath, with a sock, with a shoe, and bare; I touched it and felt it at the heel, at the sole, toe by toe, nail by nail; I examined it both dry and sweaty, both warm and cold, both tired and rested; in the end I realized that I might spend not merely a year but my whole life studying it without coming to any conclusion, and so I went over, provisionally, to my right foot. This I am still studying, and I don't know how long this may take me because I have ascertained that the right foot is much more difficult to get to know than the left. Usually people believe that the two feet are identical; well, it's a mistaken idea. In the first place the left foot is on the left and the right foot on the right; in the second place, the two feet never do the same thing, for if one moves the other stays still, if one is in the air the other rests on the ground. From this arise a number of differences which it would take too long to list in detail.

Now if the feet, which are obviously a fairly simple part of the body, are so hard to explain, what will happen to me when I reach my head which is so much more complicated and mysterious? Yes, getting to know oneself is really not easy, even for someone like myself who has practically nothing to do. Nevertheless, cost what it may, it is necessary to know oneself. Otherwise there is the possibility that one may become a stranger to oneself, as happened to me some years ago: I woke up with a start, in pitch darkness, on the pallet in my hut, and took hold, with my right hand, of a hand which was moving at the head of the bed, and, thinking it was someone else's hand, I was terrified, and then I twisted a finger of this hand violently and almost fainted with pain because the hand was my own. It was in fact this incident that decided me to embark upon a serious attempt at self-knowledge. For what in the world would have happened if I had mistaken my own head for someone else's and if, for instance, I had tried to put out my eyes or strangle myself?

One's body, in any case, does not allow itself to be forgotten. When I least expect it, it reminds me of its existence in two ways, both of them, if you come to think of it, strange, since both of them are disagreeable and inopportune—hunger and cold. Never, never does my body call attention to itself by any pleasing sensation. Luckily it's not difficult: it swallows anything, the leavings from the dustbins, rotten fruit and vegetables in the markets, scraps from the slaughterhouse; and it resigns itself, with the same indifference, to being covered with torn and stinking rags. The only trouble is that I do not always manage to establish a relationship between hunger and food, between cold and clothes or a fire; and so what very often happens is that I spend whole days huddled in the dark in my hut, vainly wondering what is needed to get rid of the sensation of hunger and cold. I go on wondering for a long time but discover nothing, and in the end I get confused in the head and doze off, only to awaken some hours later still with the same problem: what is it that gets rid of hunger? What is it that gets rid of the cold? It may seem strange, but sometimes the answer comes to me from the beasts and birds, the dogs and cats which are the only inhabitants of this lonely river-bank where I have built my hut. I recollect that one day, after seeing a dog burrowing in a rubbish-heap and then gnawing a bone, it occurred to me to do the same, so I picked up a carob-pod that was lying near by, gnawed it and chewed it and found that gradually, as I swallowed it, my hunger diminished. For that day the problem of hunger was therefore solved. But next day I had already forgotten this sensible solution, and as hunger attacked me I racked my brains in vain for a way in which to satisfy it.

It may be thought, perhaps, that I am, as they say, a bit crazy. But that is not so; I am always in full possession of my faculties. And here is a proof of it. A few days ago I was on the point of discovering who I was before I became what I am now. As usual, I had seen something which was familiar to me and which I seemed to have already seen and experienced in, so to speak, another life; and I wanted to tell Luigino about it. He is a down-and-out like me, except that he is yellow and thin and wrinkled while I am plump and bulky and rubicund. We were sitting in the sun on the rocks of the river-bank, and suddenly I said to him: "Today I saw a first-class funeral."

"Why first-class?" asked Luigino.

I explained to him that when a hearse is adorned with angels and gilt columns it means it is first-class. Then I went on: "You may not believe it, but I felt that I had seen this funeral before, that it wasn't new to me."

"So what?"

"So I understood that I had died, I don't know when, and that I'd been carried round the town in a funeral procession just like this one."

Luigino made no objection. He is a man who is not interested in deeds, only in words. For example, if somebody says to him: "Luigino, today's Tuesday", he, instead of answering that it's not Tuesday but Wednesday, will ask: "And what does Tuesday mean?" thus reducing everyone to silence because it is obvious that the word "Tuesday", taken by itself, means nothing. So now again he did not find any fault with my hypothesis of being already dead; all he did was to ask: "Dead? What does 'dead' mean?"

I was disconcerted, but finally, with a supreme effort, I managed to reply: "Dead is the opposite of alive."

"And alive, what does 'alive' mean?"

"The opposite of dead."

But he was not satisfied with these answers, and so a discussion followed and in the end I was no longer so very sure of having been dead because I no longer knew what the word meant; and the whole thing ended with a great burst of anger. Oh yes, because if I had really known that I had been dead, I might perhaps also have been able to know for certain that I had been alive. But, not knowing this, I was left doubting whether I had ever lived, whether I had ever existed, whether I had ever been here.

# Signs

I left the house with the feeling, at the same time both precise and obscure, that something unusual had happened, or was happening, to me; once I was on the embankment by the Tiber I turned to look: smooth and yellowish, with balconies in the shape of soap-dishes and windows surrounded by a narrow frame of travertine, the small block of flats really had nothing abnormal about it. Or rather, there *was* something unusual: the shutters on the first floor, all of them without exception, were closed. I wondered if this was what had troubled me but concluded that it was not; and I started walking along beside the parapet above the river.

Again there was nothing unusual about the row of buildings, all of them rather similar to the one out of which I had come, lined up, as far as the eye could see, along the pavement, in a perspective of yellow and grey façades and massive balconies; nor yet in the numbed, purplish winter sky; nor in the asphalt of the road, grey and smooth with iridescent patches of motor oil here and there; nothing unusual along the whole of the Lungotevere except for at least six small cars of the same make and the same light colour passing along it one after the other. Even the trunks and the white-speckled branches of the plane-trees, with a few rusty leaves clinging to them here and there, looked to me normal; but I noticed that in every three plane-trees there was one that was decidedly smaller, and I wondered what this could mean. As I walked, I followed the course of the river with my eye: yellow in colour and glossy, like the belly of a toad, the Tiber would have appeared to be motionless if there had not been thin, black branches in it at intervals, caught up in its wrinkled waters and slipping swiftly by, giving the sense of the current's motion. Here again there was nothing unusual, apart from the fact that I counted nine of these branches. There had been three of the smaller plane-trees and six of the cars which were all alike, and now there were nine branches: it seemed to me that there was something not very clear, or rather all too clear, in this progression. Meanwhile I went on walking and arrived at an open space in front of the approach to a bridge.

In the middle of this space there were the trees and bushes of a little public garden; all round, on the ground floors of the houses, various shops, and on the pavement a petrol pump. I looked very carefully at this open space to see if there was anything unusual there but did not notice anything. Beside the pump a car was having its tank filled up by two attendants. Now the pump was painted green, the attendants' clothes were green, and the car was also green; suddenly all this green made me suspicious, and I went over and heard the following dialogue:

"Shall we put in anti-freeze?"

"No, thanks."

"But last night the temperature went down to below freezing-point."

"But I put my car in a garage at night."

"In that case, I say no more."

I left the petrol-pump and went, shop by shop, round the open space. There was a café, a large, very ordinary café, with three windows full of sweets and bottles, and a counter

c*

73

with the usual bits of coloured crockery. There were only two customers there, drinking coffee at the counter with their backs turned to the door. They were both wearing similar light brown camel-hair overcoats; but even this, unusual though it was, was still not the unusual thing that was troubling me. I looked at myself for a moment in the looking-glass of the café and saw that I had a broad red stain on the right cuff of my shirt, corresponding with the inside surface of my wrist. I am a clean man, although poor; and I felt I must get rid of this stain as soon as possible. But how? There were only two solutions: either to wash out the stain at once, or to go home and change my shirt. I decided to wash out the stain, because I live in the suburbs, a very long way away; and indeed, on the far side of the open space, I saw, written up in large white letters, the word "Chemist". I went across and, to save time, walked through the public garden.

Here I noticed something really strange; in the garden there were four seats and on each seat a couple: so far, so good. But the man in each couple was a soldier; and this seemed to me altogether too much. What did it mean? Ruminating over this problem, I reached the pavement opposite and went into the chemist's shop.

It was a long, narrow place, garishly lit, with a counter at the far end and the shelves on its four walls full of twinkling bottles. The person in charge, a woman of about fifty with a crudely made-up face and a pyramid of raven hair on the top of her head, welcomed me with a questioning look in her round, black eyes. The following dialogue took place between us:

"I want some soap to wash out this stain."

"I don't sell that kind of soap. I only have toilet soap."

"Why, what sort of soap would be needed?"

"Laundry soap. Or it would be still better for you to change your shirt. How d'you mean to wash it? The blood has soaked into the material."

"But won't a piece of toilet soap wash out the stain just the same?"

"Yes, it's possible, but it won't do it so well as laundry soap."

"Well, give me a piece of toilet soap."

During this conversation I noticed another thing which was truly suspicious: the woman had a wide low-necked dress which left the top part of her bosom visible. And, right between the twin swellings of her breasts, she had pinned to the edge of her dress an enamel brooch of exactly the same green colour as the petrol-pump, the attendants' clothes and the car which I had observed shortly before. A mere coincidence? I took the piece of soap, paid for it, went out and walked over to the café.

I entered, asked the way to the lavatory and shut myself in it with relief. But my feeling of relief did not last long: the floor-tiles were also green, just like the woman's brooch, the petrol-pump and the car. Uneasily I took off my overcoat, my jacket and my pullover and hung them all up on the hooks. Then I turned on the tap, dipped my cuff into the water and started rubbing it vigorously. As I was washing the stain I noticed another unusual thing: in the wall there was a crack that had more or less the shape of a man standing up; and if I placed myself in a certain position my shadow fitted in almost exactly with the crack. Was this too a mere coincidence? I finished washing the cuff, for better or worse, drained off the reddened, frothy water, dressed again and went out, leaving the soap beside the wash-basin. Once outside the café, I was nevertheless forced to recognize that all my efforts at washing had served no

75

purpose: the stain, even though paler, was still there and the wet cuff round my wrist caused me discomfort.

Then I had an idea: I would buy a shirt and change the garment on the spot, actually in the shop. No sooner said than done: I turned into a broad street leading out of the little square and, a few steps further on, came upon the shop I was wanting. I went in; the place was empty; the assistant, an exceedingly slim young man with a face as white as paper and a bow tie at his long, thin neck, asked me earnestly:

"What can I do for you?"

This was our conversation:

"I want a shirt."

"Zephyr or poplin?"

"Zephyr."

"White or coloured?"

"Coloured."

"What size do you take?"

"42, I think."

"Here are some very smart shirts. Broad stripes, narrow stripes, plain-coloured."

"I'll take this one. Can I put it on at once?"

He seemed a little surprised at my request; but he opened the door of a small dressing-room and, after turning on the light, left me. The feeling of something unusual that was happening to me or had already happened was now so strong and so painful that, after I had undressed, I sat down, half-naked, on a stool and burst into tears. I went on crying for a minute and then, even in this dressing-room, I noticed a very suspicious thing: three strips of the wooden floor had become detached and I was in fact able to raise them with my hand, all three of them. Again the number three. I was frightened and tried to raise a fourth strip, but could not succeed in doing so: there were three of them, and three they had to remain. I put on the new shirt, dressed again, rolled up the old shirt and left the dressing-room.

At the moment of paying, I put my hand in my pocket, remembering that I had a five thousand lire note; instead, I found a bundle of ten thousand lire notes that I did not recollect possessing. I handed one of these notes to the assistant, but he handed it back to me, pointing out that it was stained with blood at one corner. I gave him a clean one and thought to myself: "What a fuss about a dirty note! And he doesn't realize that those strips of wood in the floor of his dressing-room might be a serious, a very serious thing." Then he made a parcel of the old shirt, handed it to me, ran and opened the door with a bow, and I left the shop.

I went back to the little square and from there took my way again along the Lungotevere. I no longer had that very uncomfortable feeling of something wet round my wrist; but the sense of some unusual happening in which I was caught, as in a trap, still persisted. As I walked, I noticed that on the Lungotevere the signs were multiplying: cars of the same make and the same colour shot past in rapid succession; a black and white bird, probably a magpie, perched on the bough of a plane-tree, and then, a few plane-trees farther on, another bird, a black one, possibly a raven, also on a bough; three children with their mother, all three of them wearing caps of that same fatal green; three loose paving-stones exactly like the three strips of wood in the floor of the dressing-room, etc., etc. Alarmed, frightened, I stopped for just a moment in front of the yellowish block of flats which I had left not long before. There was a small crowd round the entrance-door; two police cars were standing beside the kerb; and I heard the following dialogue :

"What's happened?"

"An elderly lady has been murdered."

"Who killed her?"

"Goodness knows."

"And how was she killed?"

"Stabbed, apparently."

At any other time I should have stayed to listen because, after all, it was an interesting affair; but that feeling of something unusual that was happening to me made me hasten my step. My mind was occupied with something other than old ladies stabbed to death. Another bird, a brown one this time, was sitting on the bough of a plane-tree a little farther on. That made three. It flew away, and then I started to run, following it with my eyes as it plunged into the sky, looking as if it were falling backwards, becoming smaller and smaller, more and more remote, a black speck in the vast grey space. I was running and weeping; and I ran and wept until the bird had disappeared completely.

# You know me, Carlo

I went to convey my best wishes for Christmas to my dear friend Carlo, a man of my own age who lives with his family in a flat in the Parioli district. This has become a habit; during the year we do not see one another but at Christmas I go to convey my best wishes. Dear Carlo: we were together in our youth and then we lost sight of one another. But ten years ago we met again, when he was fifty and I was fifty; and since then, every Christmas, I go and give him my best wishes. It is a habit, as I said; and, judging at least from the way in which he welcomes me, it is a habit not only for me but, by this time, for him also.

As I was saying, on Christmas Eve I left home to go and give him my best wishes. I live in the suburbs, and I do not hesitate to admit that my house is very different from Carlo's: call it a hut rather than a house and you will have a pretty exact idea of it.

Standing among a great many other huts with its back against the wall of the Mandrione aqueduct, my hut is not lacking in the indispensable conveniences: a little minor hut arranged as a lavatory; a cooking-stove with a gas-cylinder; a floor made of real bricks; a window with panes of real glass; a roof of real tiles. How long have I lived in this hut? That is a mystery. How did I come to be there? Another mystery. Where did I live before? Yet another mystery. Anyhow, even if I've lost my memory, it doesn't mean that

79

I'm nobody. I am called, or rather they call me, Tullio; and if someone in that conglomeration of huts calls out: "Professor!", it is I who turn round to answer and no one else. Professor of what, I do not know; but Professor it is, none the less.

Christmas Eve was a really unpleasant day, with a combination, rare in Rome, of cold and damp, of frost and rain. My wife Evelina herself wrapped a woollen scarf round my neck, fastened the top button of my overcoat and placed an umbrella in my hand. The scarf was full of holes, the overcoat had a tear in the shape of a "z" right on the chest, and one of the ribs of the umbrella stuck out rebelliously. "Why," I said, "do I have to dress in rags like this? Tell me why." "To arouse pity," she answered. "And remember to say that your wife is in hospital with a serious illness; don't forget." I said nothing; I shrugged my shoulders and went out into the pouring rain.

In the bus I sat beside a window all dimmed with rain, my umbrella between my legs, my face turned towards the pane of glass. What was I thinking about? I was thinking that the thing that had brought Carlo and me together again was precisely that thing which *can* bring together two men of different financial status—and that is, culture. And this was what Evelina, with her incredibly uncouth, elementary, illiterate personality, was unable to understand. According to her, when I went to see Carlo I ought to put out my hand imploringly, as professional beggars do: charity, for the love of God! That a man should turn to another for help in the name of cultural solidarity—that she could not understand. For her, the only relationship between myself and Carlo could be the relationship between the rich man and the poor man, between the man who doles out charity and the man who receives it. Yet it was not like that: Carlo and I had been together in our younger days, working side by side in some important cause, in something of benefit to humanity, in something cultural, in fact. What this thing was in which, as equals, we had collaborated and for which we had struggled, I was quite unable to recall, owing to my usual feebleness of memory. That there had been such a thing, however, there could be no possible doubt; otherwise, when I had made myself known to Carlo ten years before, why had he not cried out: "Get away, I don't know you, I've never seen you?"

The trouble, however, was that not merely did I not know what we had done together in our younger days, but, logically, I did not know who he was nor what he did. I knew only that he was called Carlo, the name by which I had addressed him when I had met him ten years before and which must be his correct name because he had made no protest; moreover I had tried several times, with delicacy and caution, to discover his surname and his profession, but had never made any progress. I ought to have asked him this at the beginning, frankly admitting my loss of memory; now, after ten years, it was too late.

At this point I said to myself that today I would make a last attempt; goodness me, I could not go on like this, accepting clothes, money and food once a year without knowing who was giving them to me and in the name of what. Of course I must not offend his sensibilities by letting him think that for ten years I had been play-acting; but today, unobtrusively, today I must, yes, I *must* arrive at the truth.

This decision made me feel better—to such a degree that I purposely left in the bus the umbrella with the rebellious rib which Evelina had given me in order to inspire pity, and, once I was in the street, I pulled from my neck the tattered scarf—another stimulus to compassion—and threw

81

it into the gutter. I did not wish to arouse pity and I did not want charity. I wanted to meet, as man to man, a friend, and to recall together the good days of our youth and our glorious collaboration.

I reached the building in which he lived—which, alas, had no porter; I went up in the lift and came to his door—which, alas, had no nameplate. While the maid went to look for him, I looked round the entrance-hall in the hope of seeing something from which I might at least deduce his profession. But no, there was nothing : a console table with a looking-glass; four chairs; a few framed prints; an umbrella-stand. Truly a mysterious man, a man who concealed (but for what purpose?) his own personality. And yet, when he came in, there were the usual greetings: "Carlo, I've come to wish you a happy Christmas. Allow me to embrace you." "Good old Tullio, I'm delighted to see you; thank you for coming."

We were silent for a moment, looking at one another; then, not without some embarrassment, I said : "Listen, Carlo, let's go for a moment into your study. I have something to say to you."

You must note that I said "study" deliberately. If he had a study, I was already one step forward, for it would mean that he studied something. Otherwise he would have answered : "I haven't a study, I have a laboratory, a consulting-room, a library"; and then I should have known that he was a scientist, a doctor, a man of letters. But he said nothing; after looking at me for a moment in a strange manner, he merely invited me, by a gesture, towards one of the doors in the entrance-hall. I went in and found myself in a nondescript sitting-room; he pointed to an armchair, sat down opposite to me and looked at me again, with the air of a man prepared to listen. More and more embarrassed, I said: "Carlo, I'm a professor. At least, that's what they call me."

"Yes, I know."

"You know me, Carlo. You know that culture has been, and is, my speciality."

"Yes, you'd told me that, too."

"What would humanity be without culture, Carlo? A grey mass, in which the only differences would be those of money. You who are rich and I who am poor, you who give charity, I who receive it. Fortunately, there is culture."

"Yes, fortunately."

"And so our relationship is not that of a rich man and a poor man, but that of two men who in their youth have struggled together, have collaborated, have joined forces in order to attain a common cultural end."

"Well said."

I became suddenly aware that I had not yet accomplished anything. I tried to press him closely. "You had the success which in any case you deserved," I said; "I, on the other hand . . . Yet just the same, when I see you again, it seems to me only yesterday that we were carrying out our experiments together in the same laboratory . . ."

He didn't blink an eyelid. "Yes," he said, "to me it seems only yesterday, too."

I was conscious that I had started to sweat under my heavy overcoat, from embarrassment. I felt I had made a mistake, and corrected myself. "That we were working in the same library," I said.

"Yes, that's it."

"I meant to say: that we collaborated in the writing of that . . . that . . . that text."

"Yes, Tullio," he said, "what you say is true."

"Our collaboration lasted only a short time, Carlo, never-

83

theless it can't be denied that we contributed, to a degree that was perhaps not altogether contemptible, to the progress of humanity . . ."

I looked at him: he was listening to me with half-closed eyes. I went on: "I myself, Carlo, am of course no longer what I once was. Yet these memories re-awaken old enthusiasms in me. Ah well, Carlo, we were a well-assorted couple. You remember when we published our . . . our . . . you know, that thing that we wrote together . . . you remember what an effect, in fact what a scandal . . .? Ah, Carlo, culture advances by scandals of that kind. Inevitably, every discovery endangers assured positions, established interests, conservative attitudes . . . But we did not shrink, eh, Carlo?— we did not hesitate . . ."

I realized that I did not know what more to say; my head was empty and I was damp with sweat. He, on the other hand, was calm and reserved as he watched me without speaking. We remained silent for a moment; then he looked at his watch and said: "Well, I'm sorry, but I have things to do. Thank you for coming to wish me a happy Christmas, and I wish the same to you with all my heart. And now this young lady will show you out"—and he indicated the maid who, it seemed, had been standing there beside the door during the whole of our conversation— "and she will give you the usual Christmas parcel."

Bewildered, I rose to my feet and cried: "I don't want any parcels from someone who . . . someone who . . . someone who stole my idea and passed it off as his own and succeeded in making a career for himself by these means."

It was a last attempt to dislodge him, to force him to say who he was and, by implication, who *I* was. But alas, I had to deal with a type of man that did not easily betray himself. Coldly, he said: "Ah, so that's how it is, is it?

84

But when you telephoned this morning you did not think of it like that."

"I've changed my mind."

"Well, never mind. Luisa, show the gentleman to the door, will you?" So I found myself outside the flat again and went down, in bewilderment, to the street. It was raining cats and dogs; the rain was cold, and it cleared my mind. I went in again, took the lift and rang at the door. Luisa came.

"A happy Christmas to you. Have you anything for a poor old man who lives in a hut and whose wife is in hospital?"

She said nothing; she vanished, and in a short time came back with a big brown paper parcel tied up with string. "Here you are," she said. "I did it up myself, with my own hands. There's a complete suit, and two bottles, and some assorted sweets. Is that all right?"

"Thank you, thank you, thank you. And again, best wishes."

But in the street, as I walked along hurriedly in the rain, I said to myself: "What was the point of telling the truth? You were so and so; I am so and so. At least, now I should know who he is and, above all, who I myself am."

# The Judas Tree

I tried, this morning, to slip out through the entrance-hall; but my father called me, from his study : "Adalberto, come here!"

I went in. He was standing behind his handsome nineteenth-century desk, a suitable desk for a confidential lawyer to good Roman families : small, minute in fact, he was wearing a double-breasted suit of heavy English cloth with green and crimson stripes on a grey ground, and his light blue eyes were like holes in his earth-coloured face. Crestfallen, I said : "Good morning, did you call me?"

He replied with a calmness that I at once felt to be excessive : "Yes, I called you. Look, the clerk isn't here, he's ill. Will you be so kind as to take these registered letters to the post office? And then—here's the money—buy me four packets of cigarettes, my usual ones."

I said submissively : "Very well", and put out my hand to take the envelopes and the money. Then, all of a sudden, he banged his fist on the desk and shouted : "So you agree without a murmur to act as my clerk. You don't protest, you don't tell me to go to hell. And there's a reason, which is that, though you're more than twenty-eight, you haven't even got a degree and you do nothing and you don't want to do anything and you're a first-class idler. And I've been slaving all my life to bring up—what? A clerk, an errand-boy, a man who's good for nothing but to post letters and to go to the tobacconist's and buy cigarettes."

I looked at him while he was shouting, at his face, blood-congested beneath the yellow skin, at his blue eyes, inflamed and seeming to bulge with rage, at his lips drawn back over his nicotine-darkened teeth; and as I looked at him I was almost diverted, so fascinated was I by his anger. Perhaps he noticed this because, suddenly, he shouted: "Get out, get out, get out!" I did not let him say this twice. I put out my hand, seized the letters and ran off, pursued even as far as the staircase by ferocious yells: "Get out, get out!"

Once in the street, I slackened my pace and started walking in a leisurely way towards the post office building in Piazza Mazzini. As I walked I thought about my father and his outbursts of rage, and I asked myself in genuine astonishment: "How on earth does he come to be convinced that I do nothing, whereas I myself have the impression that I am busy, extremely busy, and that I toil almost to the limit of my strength?"

I lit a cigarette and looked all round me, and all of a sudden I understood: living, or rather being conscious, at every moment of one's life, that one was alive, was for me a great thing, in fact it was too much. In such conditions work would have been a supplementary fatigue that I did not feel able to face. The better to explain to myself this reflection, I took as an example the picture galleries that one spends two or three hours going round, examining the pictures one by one, and then one is dead tired, exhausted, utterly destroyed, and one hurries home and throws one-self on the bed and is unable to move. Life was like that, at any rate for me: a gallery of pictures through which I walked and walked, and the mere fact of looking at them took all the strength out of me, and there was no energy left for doing what my father called work.

In the midst of these thoughts I turned into a wide,

straight avenue, and I realized that things were just like that. Here was the street, for instance : the polished asphalt, of a pinkish grey; the two rows of tall trees, possibly poplars, all covered with the tiny, bright buds of spring; the houses, yellow, red or white; the shops on the ground floors, the shop windows, and in the shop windows the goods for sale; the passers-by, their clothes, their faces; up above, between the roofs, the spring sky with clouds gilded by the sunshine and edged with grey, moving with the wind, like the intestines of a belly in tumult, and an aeroplane, or rather a biplane, popping out of these clouds; and finally, as I lowered my eyes, the almost blue slabs of the pavement, and on these paving-stones white cigarette-ends crushed amongst black ash, and here and there yellow spittle, or dogs' excrement, brown or black, and between the joins of the paving-stones a few blades of green grass, and along the wall an ant dragging, all by itself, goodness knows where to, a gigantic piece of straw . . .

All these things and an enormous number of other things occupied me, absorbed me, captured me, each on its own account, beating with closed fists at the doors of my senses, claiming, demanding my attention. Where, in the midst of all this confusion, could I find the time to devote myself to work? And why indeed should I do so?

At this point, I do not know why, I looked up towards a row of windows on the ground floor of the building below which I was walking at that moment; I saw someone looking out from behind the glass and quickened my pace, but in vain. A minute or two later I heard the well-known voice calling me : "Adalberto !"

Resigned, I stopped and said : "Hallo, Sofia."

She ran after me, her long hair, loose on her thin shoulders and round her plump face, bobbing up and down as she moved. "What a coincidence!" she said as she caught up with me; "I came out to buy the newspapers and I run into you!"

"You liar, you know that I pass by here every morning at this time; you were at the window and as soon as you saw me you rushed out into the street."

She didn't deny it, but quickened her step, put her hand under my arm and pressed close to me. "D'you know," she said, "you're a strange kind of lover?"

"Why, how do lovers behave?"

"D'you know, you haven't yet given me a kiss that's really a kiss?"

I looked at her sideways; it seemed to me that in her place I saw my father when he was shouting at me that I did nothing. She too, in fact, was finding fault with me for doing nothing; and she wanted me to do something, to do precisely what everybody else did, in our case, lovers. I said sharply: "Be content with my loving you in my own way."

"And what is your own way?"

I stopped and, by a sudden inspiration, explained things to her. "My way of loving is knowing that you're there, being aware that you exist. At this moment, for instance, four of my five senses are busy, so to speak, registering your existence. I see you, I see your round face, a bit puffy, rather pale, with a small, curly nose, a capricious mouth, big dark eyes somewhere between grey and green and with two black scratch-marks below the eyelids: *sight*. I hear your voice, which is pleasant to listen to, sing-song, too melodious: *hearing*. I smell the sharp, rather wild smell, something between a wild animal and an old carpet, of your hair that you don't wash often enough: *the sense of smell*. On my arm I feel the grasp of your bony hand, with its long

89

fingers hooked like the claws of a kite: *the sense of touch.* What more do you want? The sense of taste does not come into it because you're not a thing that one can put into one's mouth to get its flavour; but apart from that, at this moment at least, I'm completely absorbed by you, so to speak."

"A fine sort of love. Sight, hearing, touch, smell: you're a sensualist, that's all. Besides, it's not true that I don't wash my hair. I was at the hairdresser's only yesterday morning."

"I'm not a sensualist. I don't perceive you with my senses, rather I perceive that I perceive you, that is, I perceive that you exist, that you're there, that you're present in front of me, in flesh and blood. To me, this means a great deal, a very great deal. We don't in fact do anything, and yet I'm already dead tired, exhausted. You kill me, Sofia, by the sole fact of being there, of existing; and you want me to give you a kiss into the bargain: impossible."

I had spoken in a playful tone; but what I said had a foundation of seriousness. And she understood that I was serious, for she made a grimace, moved away from me and cried: "I, on the other hand, feel that you're not there, that you don't exist, that you're not present, even in a small degree. Good-bye." With these words she turned her back on me and went away.

I should have liked to call out to her to turn back again, but I restrained myself. As I had told her, I was tired, extremely tired, anyhow of her; for that day, this might well be enough. At that moment a young, untidy-looking rag-and-bone man, slowly pedalling his tricycle with a little cart behind it in which were a few empty bottles and rags and a couple of broken umbrellas, came across the street, crying in a doleful voice: "Any old rags and bottles?"; and then, for some reason, it came into my head to make a comparison between him and a magnificent Judas tree growing at the edge of the pavement and standing out against the stormy sky, itself almost astonished, one might think, by the intense, staring violet colour of its own flowers; and I seemed to realize that I was far closer to the tree than to the man. The latter had renounced the consciousness of living in order to act, that is, to trail from one end of the city to the other, buying and selling old junk; the former, on the other hand, stood still and did nothing, or rather confined itself to feeling that it existed and that the world existed around it, and this was sufficient for it. Yes indeed, for to feel that one exists and that the world exists is a great effort; and if one makes this effort, one cannot make that other effort which consists in going round buying and selling rags, empty bottles and broken umbrellas. One has, in brief, to choose.

By now I had reached the post office building. But a swift thought caused me to turn round and walk back towards home, without either stamping or posting my father's letters. I did not even go into the tobacconist's to buy the cigarettes, I went straight on. I ran up to our flat and went into the study. My father was sitting in front of an open ledger, a cigarette between two fingers, his head bent. I threw down the envelopes and the money on his desk and said: "You see, I haven't posted the letters and I haven't bought the cigarettes. Here you are, here are the letters and the money."

To my surprise, this time he did not fly into a rage. Without looking up, he enquired: "Why?"

"Why? Because I don't feel like acting as a messenger-boy. I don't want to do anything."

"Nothing?"

"Nothing, really nothing, absolutely nothing."

"Very well. But a person who does nothing, *is* nothing; don't you think so?"

"I don't agree."

"And so, from now onwards, I shall consider you to be nothing. You know what that means?"

"I don't know and I don't wish to know."

"It means that from now onwards I shall behave as though you didn't exist, as though you weren't there."

I reflected that these were, almost exactly, the words Sofia had used; and I went out softly, in silence. I went to my room, threw myself on the bed and fell asleep almost at once, exhausted by the fatigues of this early part of the day. I slept badly, though soundly, with clenched fists and clenched teeth, closing my eyes tightly as an oyster closes its valves, my knees drawn up against my chest; and finally I awoke without feeling at all rested, feeling, in fact, dead tired. Even sleeping, then, was a fatigue, since in sleep— and especially in sleep—the consciousness of being alive went on revolving and pulsating, like a mill which is never lacking in corn to be ground. And to think that for Sofia and for my father I did not exist! I felt tired, however, of this existence of mine that was so incessant and so crowded; and so, to rest from my weariness, I fell asleep again.

# Don't let's be Dramatic

What's the use of despairing? The day after my wife's death I at once said to Eunice, my old servant who had never got on with her and couldn't endure her and nevertheless thought that she ought to put on an appropriate expression: "Above all, don't let's be dramatic. My wife is dead, that's true, but life has to go on as it did in the past, without any change."

And so I did things I was accustomed to do every day when she was alive. I went to my office, dealt with various jobs during the morning, went out before one o'clock, bought the Sicilian cake she liked so much at the pastrycook's opposite the building where my office is, even purchased a bunch of anemones, her favourite flowers, from the florist at the corner of the street. In fact the florist said to me: "How is the Signora? It's some time since we've seen her"; and I, almost in spite of myself, replied: "She's all right, thank you."

I went back home, handed over the cake to Eunice and myself saw that the anemones were put in a vase on *her* dressing-table; then, slipping into an old habit without realizing it, I said: "Eunice, serve the lunch without waiting for the Signora who, I am afraid, will be a bit late today." Eunice gave me an odd look, but she said nothing and shortly afterwards came back into the dining-room and laid another place beside mine.

Later I sat down all alone at the over-large table in the

dining-room that had once echoed to her chatter; and I looked with some bewilderment at her empty place and it seemed to me that I saw her there in front of me, blonde and pale, contemplating me with her huge, rather sad blue eyes and saying to me : "What's the matter with you today? You seem rather strange;" and I was almost on the point of answering her : "I quite believe I'm rather strange : you are dead." But then the servant came in to tell me that someone was wanting me. I thought she meant on the telephone, and said : "You know that when I'm at meals, I don't answer telephone calls;" but Eunice replied : "They're not on the telephone but in the entrance-hall."

"Who is it?"

"A girl."

"And what does she want?"

"She says she's come about a job."

"Ah yes, I'll come at once."

I rose and went out into the hall. She was sitting in a corner, on the edge of a chair; when she saw me, she rose to her feet. I noticed immediately that she was not at all like my wife : my wife had been very fair, this one had brown hair; my wife had been thin, pale, delicate-looking, whereas this girl was dark-skinned, rather plump and coarse-looking; my wife had been elegant and aristocratic, this girl was simple and plebeian. My wife had been thirty; this girl was barely twenty. My wife looked, and had indeed been, a lady; this girl looked like a street-urchin, a gutter-snipe, a vagabond.

In her way of dressing, too, she bore no resemblance whatever to my wife. The latter dressed well, too well even, always in town clothes, always like a sophisticated married woman, with silk stockings, stiletto-heeled shoes, light silk dresses in sober colours, elaborate jewellery and hair styles. This

94

girl, on the other hand, was a real ragamuffin, with a high-necked sweater up to her ears, a torn coat, a very short skirt. Wollen stockings up to her knees, men's shoes, a plastic handbag and no gloves on her red, swollen hands. My wife, finally, was always spotless, carefully made-up, scented. This one had a mass of rumpled hair, lips awkwardly smeared with red, and I could not make out whether her round cheeks were sunburnt or dirty.

And yet, in spite of all these differences, I could not help saying to her, as soon as I came into the entrance-hall: "You've come after that job? Let me have a look at you."

I took her by the hand and made her move round the room. She submitted, somewhat surprised. I said finally: "I think you'll do. Now tell me, what's your name?"

"My name's Maura."

My wife's name was Elisabetta, a name very different from Maura. "Now, Maura," I said, "Come with me."

She gave me another curious look, but said nothing and followed me. I led her down the passage towards the bedroom. I had not slept there the previous night; I had arranged myself as best I could on the sofa in the drawing-room. I went in, turned on the light and said: "Come on, come along in, make yourself at home, Maura."

She walked on tip-toe across the olive-green pile carpet, then looked round. "What a lovely room," she said.

"Yes, this is our bedroom. Now come here, Maura, just for a moment."

From the bedroom I went on into the bathroom. In front of the window was my wife's dressing-table. "Sit down here."

She sat down. I took a bottle of eau-de-Cologne and a wad of cotton-wool and quickly started cleaning her up. The cotton-wool, passed delicately over her neck and cheeks,

95

became dark in colour: she was not sunburnt, she was dirty. I lifted her hair: she had small ears, round and perfect but of a curious colour like the yolk of an egg: I cleaned them too. Then I sat down in front of her, armed with a lipstick, and with a few strokes painted her lips. I touched up her eyes with a black pencil; I put a thin veil of pale powder on her cheeks. "Now let's go over there."

She looked astonished but did not breathe a word. I went to the big built-in wardrobe and threw open the doors. Elisabetta had a great quantity of clothes: hanging there in a row, pressed closely one against another, were numbers of dresses of all shapes and materials—two-piece and one-piece dresses, in wool, in silk, in muslin, in cotton, black, plain-coloured, multi-coloured, with patterns on them and without. I searched for a moment, then pulled out a red woollen coat and skirt and threw them on the bed: "Put that on," I told her. Then, from amongst the shoes lined up below the dresses, I chose a pair of low-heeled country shoes; from a drawer, a pair of green woollen stockings; from another drawer, a black brassière, a black suspender-belt, a black petticoat; from a third drawer, a grey vest; and I placed the things all together beside the coat and skirt. "Change completely," I said; "I'm going out of the room. Call me when you've finished."

She opened her eyes wide in astonishment as she stood in front of the clothes, putting out a timid hand to touch them. "Now hurry up," I went on; "lunch is ready." Out in the passage I rubbed my hands together and started walking up and down, feeling well pleased. Suddenly an idea came into my head and I went back into the room without knocking. There was a cry: "One moment, I've got nothing on."

96

"I'm not looking at you. I'd forgotten something." My head turned away, I walked over to a picture hanging on the wall near the bathroom door; I took it down, and the steel rectangle of a safe became visible. I opened it and took out, one by one, a pearl necklace, a pair of pearl earrings, a gold brooch with precious stones, two sapphire and diamond rings, Elisabetta's favourite jewels; and, placing them on the chest-of-drawers without turning round, I said : "Put these on too."

"Am I really to put them on?" she asked.

This made me angry. "If I tell you to put them on, don't argue : just do as you're told."

I left the room again and went into the dining-room. The maid was standing at the kitchen door, holding a tray. "Am I to serve the lunch?" she enquired.

"Not yet. We'll wait for the Signora."

She too gave me a strange, surprised look, but she said nothing and went back into the kitchen. Left alone, I put a Vivaldi record on the gramophone; I poured out the wine and the water into the glasses; I threw a couple of logs on the dying fire; and then I rubbed my hands together with joy and started walking up and down in front of the table. I recalled that Elisabetta, before eating, took certain medicines, so I went and fetched them from the sideboard and put them beside her plate. Then I walked up and down again, rubbing my hands together from time to time, feeling well satisfied and at the same time impatient.

Five minutes passed, ten minutes passed, then a quarter of an hour. Finally I rang the bell. "Eunice," I said, "will you go and see what the Signora is doing? Goodness me, she ought to be ready by now."

Eunice sighed, but she said nothing and went out. She reappeared a little later, stopped in the doorway and said in a curious, indulgent sort of voice: "The Signora isn't there. She's gone."

"She's gone? You mean she's gone out?"

"Yes, she's gone out."

"Oh well, I suppose she had something to do; perhaps her mother telephoned her and she had to go at once to her mother. Eunice, I think it will be better not to wait for her. I'll have lunch by myself. But keep the food hot for when the Signora returns; after all, she can't be very long."

I sat down, and Eunice held out the tray to me, with an *hors d'œuvre* of cold meats and pickles. As I helped myself, I said: "What sort of weather is it, Eunice?"

"It's raining."

"I bet the Signora's gone out without an umbrella; and then she complains that she catches colds."

"No, she's taken an umbrella; she's taken the best one, the one with a silver handle."

"Oh well, so much the better." It really was a horrible day; in the dining-room it was almost dark. I went and turned on the light and looked for a moment, from the window, at the rain that was coming down diagonally, heavy and leaden-coloured; then I went and sat down at the table again and started eating with a good appetite.

# Enrica Baile

This morning I received the following letter: "This letter comes from Venezuela and has been written by the celebrated Brango and must go all round the world you must make 24 copies and send it off, after nine days you will have a pleasant surprise. Even if you are not superstitious bear in mind what follows. Valeriano Banga, South American general, received a prize of 5,000,000 dollars, Enrica Baile of Vercelli (Colombia) received the chain-letter and threw it away, her family suffered misfortunes and lost dear ones and she became poor.

"In 1940 Walter Beroche a general in the Venezuelan army had the copies made by a secretary the reception was immediate his position became excellent. An employee received the copies he forgot to send them on he lost his job and then he decided to do them again in a few days he found himself in much better circumstances. A person at Silla received the chain-leter and threw it away after 9 days he perished in an accident. Do not break the chain."

I read the letter and fell into deep thought. How many fascinating questions were raised in these few lines! I am inclined by nature to reverie; the letter was just what was needed to make me start day-dreaming. First of all there were some mysterious coincidences: all the persons mentioned in the letter, lucky or unlucky, were in Latin America and all of them had surnames beginning with "B": Brango, Banga, Baile, Beroche. Then there was the charming imprecision of the details: the celebrated (but why celebrated?) Brango; the town of Silla (from the Roman dictator?); the prize of 5 million dollars (what prize? the prize for what?); an employee (what was his employment?); his job (but what job?): an accident (what accident?).

More than anything, however, it was the figure, barely mentioned yet so alive, of Enrica Baile which started me dreaming. Beautiful, proud, courageous, she had refused to send on copies of the letter, she had suffered misfortunes (but what misfortunes?), had lost dear ones (what dear ones?), had become poor. What had become of her? What did she do? Where was she?

My wife's voice awakened me from these day-dreamings. She came into my study crying: "There he is, smoking and dreaming when he ought to have been at work long ago! Why, what are you doing, why don't you go to the newspaper offices? D'you know it's almost four o'clock already?"

I answered quite sensibly: "I ought to be interviewing some celebrated personage who is passing through Rome. But today there's no celebrity passing through Rome. So I have nothing to do."

"Well, here's an idea: why don't you get an interview with General Banga?"

I gave a start. "Why, how d'you know?"

"Know what? There's all this fuss over this general and you're not even aware of it; you just sit there day-dreaming."

"What's the fuss?"

"Why, it's in all the papers. You're a bit vague, aren't you? Look!"

She showed me a newspaper; and indeed, on the front page, there was a big three-column headline: "Demonstrations against General Banga. The general, barricaded in his hotel, declares he will stay three days in the capital."

"Come on, pull yourself together," added my wife; "go and inteview the general."

"But it appears that he's a blood-thirsty character, responsible for the deaths of thousands of people. Besides, he's an arch-thief."

"What does that matter to you? Are you, or aren't you a journalist? Has General Banga news value, or hasn't he?"

In short, I allowed myself to be persuaded. My wife, pretending to be my secretary, telephoned the hotel and to my surprise the interview was granted immediately. Banga would expect me in an hour's time, in room no 415 at the hotel.

My wife was generous with her advice. "Take advantage of the opportunity, have an interview that will make a stir, make him tell you how many people he has made away with, how many millions he has stolen, screw all you can out of him with a bit of flattery and a few compliments. And don't pay any attention to your colleagues who set themselves up as moralists or to those other idiots who start demonstrations: it's only done from envy. There's not a single one of them that wouldn't kill and rob twice as much as the general in order to have his money. They say he's a multi-millionaire; and not just with a few millions but with hundreds of millions. Lucky man! Now put on your new blue suit, with your black shoes and white shirt and dark tie: damn it, he's a general! And don't forget to address him all the time as "Excellency", d'you see?"

So, in my blue suit, with a new notebook and a new Biro pen in my pocket, I made my way to the hotel. There, in front of the entrance, was a dark, threatening crowd, held back with difficulty by a cordon of uniformed police;

above their heads waved placards with slogans such as: "Banga Go Home"; "Down with the murderer Banga"; "Banga Out"; "Banga to the Gallows"; and so on. But, once I was inside the lobby of the hotel, I realized that its life was in no way disturbed by the demonstration. Everything was normal, the lights were lit, customers were coming and going, the little band was playing. I went over to the porter's desk, gave him my name, and was at once informed that I was expected; I was then shown to the lift which deposited me a moment later at the third floor. Endless corridors, diffused lights, thick, silent carpets; I strolled along to the door of No. 415, knocked and was bidden to come in.

I found myself in a sitting-room in the Empire style, all white and gold; a door was open, and in the adjoining room could be seen an unmade bed. Standing in the middle of the sitting-room was a dark young man with long side-whiskers and a neat moustache, who said to me: "I am the secretary. The General has just risen from his afternoon rest and is dressing. He will grant you the interview as soon as he is ready."

"Thank you."

I sat down, took out my notebook and pen; the secretary went over to the window and looked out, turning his back on me. An old man's voice, raucous, deep, full of catarrh, unsteady from age yet authoritative in character, pronounced suddenly from the adjoining room: "My boots!"

At once the secretary rushed forward and vanished into the other room. Silence followed; then: "My tunic!"

"My belt!"

"My pistol!"

"My decorations!"

"My cap!"

Again silence, an even longer silence. Finally the secretary appeared in the doorway and said: "The General is ready to give the interview."

"But where is the General?"

"The General grants interviews without appearing personally. You can ask your questions and he will reply from the bedroom."

"But why?"

"There's no 'why' about it, it just is so."

It occurred to me that the General, more feared than loved, was afraid of an attempt on his life. The secretary added hastily: "By the way, the General does not answer questions concerning problems of a political, religious, economic, social or, in general, of a public nature. The General only answers questions of a private character."

"What does 'private' imply?"

"Questions, for instance, concerning personal tastes in the fields of art, of tourism, of fashion, and so on."

"And about individuals, does the General accept questions about individuals?"

"About individuals, yes, provided they're not public figures."

So I plucked up courage and said: "In that case I should like the General to answer this question: 'Have you ever known a woman called Enrica Baile?'"

To my astonishment I heard the thick voice reply: "Yes."

"And who is Enrica Baile?"

"An unhappy wretch."

"Why an unhappy wretch?"

"Enrica's husband set himself up against me. Some of my followers broke into Baile's house by night, they used violence against Enrica, they killed her husband, her children and her servants, they set fire to the house. Excesses, no

103

doubt, but they must be seen against the background of the political struggle."

"How old was Enrica at the time?"

"Twenty-five."

"Was she beautiful?"

"Extremely beautiful. But her face was irreparably disfigured in the fire."

"And where is she now?"

"She lives in the poorest quarter of my capital."

"And what does she do?"

"She's a pauper."

"What does that imply?"

"She goes begging, she sleeps in a hut, she appeases her hunger with garbage, she dresses in rags."

Again there was a long silence. I was trying to think up a new series of questions. Finally I asked: "Excellency, do you remember ever having received a prize of five million dollars? And if you received it, what prize was it and why was it given to you?"

Anxiously I awaited his reply. Then the thick voice answered: "The prize of five million dollars was awarded to me because, in an action that lasted three months, I routed a dangerous band of terrorists entrenched in the mountains near the capital."

"And who awarded you this prize?"

"The Government."

"And who was head of the Government at that time?"

"I myself was the Head of the Government."

"But in that case it was you who awarded the prize to yourself?"

"Exactly."

I was left speechless. The secretary intervened: "The interview is finished; you can go."

"But there's something else I should like to ask."

"You can't, it's finished."

He pushed me out of the room in an ill-mannered way and there was nothing left for me but to go home. There I wrote a careful account of the interview, omitting nothing: the letter, the demonstration, the secretary, the General, Enrica Baile; and then I took it to the newspaper. But would you believe it? The editor informed me that he could not publish the interview because I had not succeeded in making the General talk about himself, but only about a certain Enrica Baile who, being a person entirely unknown, had no news value and was consequently of no interest to the paper.

# Why, who said so?

I had the following dream. I was lying on my back inside a glass box; I looked up and saw the feet of a number of people who, as they walked, passed across the lid of the box. There were women's feet and men's feet; I could distinguish between them by the shape of the soles of their shoes; I wanted to say to them: "Don't walk over me; can't you see you're walking over me?"; but no voice issued from my mouth. And now two pairs of feet, one masculine and the other feminine, stopped right on top of the lid of the box, exactly above my head. Evidently these were two people who were conversing quietly about their own affairs, a man and a woman, perhaps a young couple, and perhaps talking about love; and they had chosen precisely this place to talk about it. I wanted to say to them too: "Don't stop on top of me like this; don't you realize that I'm lying under your feet while you exchange tender remarks and make plans for the future? Don't you realize?" But again this time I could not manage to speak. Then, suddenly, something worse occurred: a very heavy, massive object, a trunk, a wardrobe, a wooden chest, was moved with great effort and fatigue to be placed on top of me and left there for ever. I heard the voices of the people who were pushing it; the enormous object was by now obscuring half of the glass; its black shadow was advancing steadily; soon I should be plunged in darkness. Then I cried out with all the breath I had in my body: "Stop, what are you doing?

I'm underneath here, don't you realize I'm here?" And I raised my hands upwards, so as to lift the lid. But it was too late; the lid wouldn't rise even the smallest part of an inch; the dark mass was advancing, it covered me, plunged me in gloom; and then I woke up with a long, bitter moan.

I knew at once that I had been dreaming I was dead, and instinctively I threw myself over to the side of the bed where my wife was sleeping. I embraced her and asked her, in a loud, clear voice: "Is it true then, have I got to die?"

She gave a groan, but I insisted: "Tell me, is it true then, have I got to die?"; and this time the answer came in a slow voice, each word pronounced distinctly: "Why, who said so?"

For a moment I thought I had not heard properly. Then, absurdly, irresistibly, an immense, even if incredulous, joy flooded my heart. I felt that perhaps it was true; perhaps, as my wife appeared to imply, I should not die, I was immortal or rather not mortal, I should not die but should go on living indefinitely. I pursued the question: "What d'you mean, who said so? Everybody says so. We all know, it's inevitable."

I got no reply. After those words that were so clear and so important, my wife, like a Sibyl who delivers her oracle and relapses into unconsciousness, had resumed her sleep, or rather her snoring—a gentle, subdued, delicate snoring, it is true, but a snoring nevertheless. For a moment I thought of awakening her; then I was afraid that this would irritate her and cause her to retract her response; and I thought it better to defer the explanation until the following morning. And so, comforted and hopeful, I went to sleep again, with the wonderful sensation that perhaps, yes, perhaps, truly, I should never die.

I awoke, as usual, about nine o'clock and immediately

recalled my dream and my wife's remark. I raised myself on my elbow; in the half-darkness I saw her sleeping, curled up on one side, her hair spread out over her bare shoulders. I placed my hand on her neck. "It's time now, you must wake up."

Slowly, dazedly, she moved, turned over, opened her eyes. "Last night," I said, "I had a nightmare."

"So what?"

"It seemed to me that I was dead; I woke up and asked you: 'Have I got to die?' and you answered: 'Why, who said so?' Now, I really want to know what you meant by that remark?"

"Go and open the window."

I got up, went to the window and pulled up the roller-shutter. Then I turned back into the room: at the far side of the bed my wife was shielding her dazzled eyes with her arm. "What's the weather like?" she enquired.

"Splendid."

"Good; then we shall be able to go for a drive."

I began again: "Last night I had a nightmare, I thought I was dead, so I asked you: 'Have I got to die?' and you . . ." but I could go no farther. My wife, with a sort of brusque violence, threw back the bedclothes, jumped out of bed and went out of the room. I followed her.

The bathroom in our flat is at the far end of the passage, opposite the bedroom. I saw my wife's pink, crumpled night-dress disappear into the bathroom, and the door was shut in my face. A moment later I heard the rush of water from the shower and, through it, the sound of my wife singing. The sound came irregularly, with high notes and low notes, as though the singer were panting and out of breath yet joyous as the rush of cold water descended upon her. Then the singing became more distinct and regular;

108

after the cold shower, my wife was now taking a warm one. Suddenly the bathroom door was thrown open; she came out in her dressing-gown and came back into the bedroom. Standing in front of the dressing-table with her back turned to me, she looked at herself for a long time in the glass, studying her face—her favourite kind of reading after waking up in the morning. I took advantage of this to say, for the third time: "Last night I had a nightmare; I woke up with a start and . . ."

But again this time I could get no further. My wife turned on the little radio on the dressing-table and set it, at full volume, to a jazz band. This was a habit of hers: to dress and undress and perform her toilet to the sound of jazz. Suddenly she turned round and cried: "Aren't you content, aren't you happy to be alive? *I* am: it's a lovely day, we're going for a drive in the country, I've had a stinging cold shower which has woken me up. Come on now, come on, let's dance."

And so—she with expert, impetuous briskness, I awkwardly and filled with embarrassment and regret—we danced in the middle of the untidy room, in front of the unmade bed. Then my wife stopped and exclaimed: "Ugh, I'm out of breath! Besides, it's late, I must get dressed."

I went to the radio, turned it off, then moved towards her as she sat on the bed, one foot in the air, putting on a stocking, and I said firmly: "Now listen to me, once and for all, and answer me, please: last night I had a nightmare, I thought I was dead, I woke up with a start and . . ."

Suddenly there was a knock at the door. My wife, naturally, called out: "Come in!"; and so once again I was left in the middle of a sentence. It was the cook, an ugly but zealous young woman, who had come to take the orders for the day. "Come in," said my wife; "come in, Egle. Well,

109

then: the Doctor and I are out to lunch today, we're going to the sea. This evening there will be four for dinner. But let me tell you at once, Egle, yesterday evening's dinner was a disaster, and if this evening's is of the same kind I shall be forced not to invite my friends any more."

"But, Signora, what disaster, where was the disaster?"

"Where was it? In the kitchen and, even before it was in the kitchen, it was inside you, Egle. The *timbale* was half raw, but to make up for that the asparagus was over-cooked. We won't mention the salad; evidently your love affairs are not going well, Egle, for you put in the salt twice over. And as for the roast . . ."

Et cetera, et cetera. Gradually, while my wife and the cook were engaged in their discussion, I slipped out of the door without their noticing it and went into the sitting-room. I put on a record of some kind, sank into an arm-chair and started listening, trying, by means of the music, to free myself of my ill humour. Then, suddenly, as I reflected on the manner in which my wife, during the night, had replied to my question about death, I saw that, fundamentally, her reply a short time before had been given in the same manner when I had repeated the same question. During the night she had said: "Why, who said so?"; now she had not answered at all, or rather she had answered by doing the things that she did every morning of her life; but, when carefully considered, the two answers resembled one another. Unconscious, ambiguous, just like the answers of a little capricious, domestic Sybil, they seemed to imply that it was useless for me to think of death, seeing that I was alive. It was a comforting answer even if modest and simple, rather like the answer a mother might have given to a child who had put to her a question like mine. But, after all, I had behaved just like a child.

110

There was a sound of doors opening and closing. My wife appeared and cried: "Well, shall we go? It's late, they're waiting for us."

We went out of the flat; in the lift my wife looked at me and said unexpectedly: "By the way, what was it you wanted to know? With so much to do, I didn't listen to you; you asked me something several times but I didn't understand properly; it was to do with something that happened last night."

"Yes," I replied, "I wanted to know if I'd woken you up. I had a nightmare and it seemed to me I'd woken you up."

"No, you didn't, I slept right through from yesterday evening until this morning. You didn't wake me up at all."

"Are you sure?"

"Absolutely sure. You didn't wake me up, I slept right through the night."

# A Thing is a Thing

We do not communicate; or rather, we communicate in a great many ways but not with words. I asked her: "What did you do this morning?" She answered: "I went for a walk." "Where?" "Round about." "Round about where?" "In the streets of the centre of the town." "But what did you do?" "I went for a walk." I remained silent for a moment, trying to transform these words mentally into images: walk, round about, streets, centre; to see my wife, that is, in the precise act of going for a walk in the streets of the centre of the town; but I saw nothing. I closed my eyes without her being aware of it, pretending to look down at my plate; I thought of her, tall, elegant, supple, with that suggestion of awkwardness and provocativeness in her narrow hips and long legs that I find so charming; I thought of her going for a walk in the streets of the centre of the town; but I saw neither her, nor the shops, nor the cars, nor the pavements, nor anything. The words meant nothing to me, they aroused no feeling in me; in fact, repeat them as I might, over and over again, they had an alarming way of changing themselves into senseless sounds.

I half-closed my eyelids and looked across at her through the pointed rays of light from the crystal of the glasses and carafes. She was wearing a blouse with yellow and orange stripes, open at the neck; all of a sudden I was struck by the intense expressiveness, not to say the disturbing quality, of one of the buttons, the top one. This button was saying,

112

in fact was shouting at me: "I am the top button of the blouse. This morning, when your wife went out, I was inserted into my button-hole; now I am outside it. It may be that I was freed from the button-hole through innocent coquettishness, so as to allow the top of her bosom to be seen; but it may also be that the blouse was unbuttoned by a quick, impatient hand, was thrown with her other garments on to a chair, in a strange room, and then, an hour or two later, put on once more and buttoned up in haste, all except the top button which was absent-mindedly left undone." A long story? And, into the bargain, maliciously detailed, a regular little narrative, or rather romance. I asked myself whether I was perhaps becoming jealous, but I quickly reassured myself. Indeed, when I looked up and raised my eyes from my wife's blouse to her face, I realized that every feature of that face, well-known as it was, conveyed to me a piece of information in which it was impossible to perceive the unconscious expression of any of my feelings. These pieces of information were, in fact, objective; they had nothing to do with me. The long, narrow, luminous grey-green eyes cried out to me: "We are the eyes"; the rather large, slightly hooked nose: "I am the nose"; the full, thick, sullen mouth: "I am the mouth." It was even embarrassing; like finding oneself in front of a shouting crowd and not knowing whom to pay attention to.

I decided to make a haphazard choice amongst all these postulants—the mouth, for example. But I immediately became aware that other messages, other pieces of information were reaching me across the space, with the quivering density and violence of arrows launched by numbers of archers: "I am the scarcely visible dark down that shadows the upper lip. I am the serious fold at the corner of the mouth. I am the clear lipstick, bright as blood. I am the

113

moist sheen, as of wet mother-of-pearl, of the teeth that can barely be seen. I am the warmth of the breath which is the cause of the tiny cracks on the lips. I am the shape of the lips, curving and compact and at the same time curiously formless. I am the little furrow above the upper lip. I am the pink tip of the tongue which at this moment is thrust a little forward so as to lick the teeth . . ." Deafened by all these tumultuous, exacting reports, I shook my head. Then I said :

"I want to make a proposal to you."

"What's that?"

"From now on, let's not talk to one another any more."

"What d'you mean, what's the matter with you?"

"I mean what I say : let's not talk to one another any more."

"But why?"

"Because there's no need for it."

"You don't love me any longer. You'd prefer me not to be there, not to exist, and as you can't make me disappear you try to make me dumb."

"On the contrary. You're so full of talk that words are now superfluous."

"No, I know what it is; you'd prefer me to be a thing just like any other thing, an object that you look at and leave where it is. You'd like me to be like that glass."

I was on the point of replying that she was infinitely more expressive and more communicative than any glass, but all of a sudden I was speechless. At her irate remark, in fact, I looked almost involuntarily in the direction of the glass and, wonder of wonders, the thing raised itself on tiptoe, so to speak, and shouted at me with all the voice it had : "I am a glass. D'you understand? I'm a glass." Confused, I paused to consider my small but presumptuous and impu-

114

dent interlocutor. When at last I recovered from my astonishment and looked up again, I saw that my wife's chair
was empty: pained and indignant, she had risen and left
the room.

Worried, I sat still, looking at the chair, wondering what
I ought to do. But suddenly that serpent of a chair—it
deserves no better name—shouted at me in an offended tone
of voice: "Why, what are you staring at? What are you
looking for? I am a chair, d'you understand? I am a chair."
And then, blindly, I fled from the room. I ran out into the
entrance-hall, opened the door and went out.

We live on the ground floor of a building which looks on
to a small public garden. Four flower-beds, four trees to
each bed. In the middle of the beds, a gravelled space with
four seats. In the centre of the space, a small fountain. I
went and sat down on one of the seats, in the shade of a
holm-oak. The garden was deserted; but the bits of paper
scattered everywhere in large quantities, the torn-up hedges,
the uprooted wire fences, the worn grass, at once cried out
at me: "This garden is deserted now because it's early afternoon. Later on it will be filled with children. All this squalor
and destruction is their doing." I pretended not to hear this
piece of information which was, in a way, depressing, and
looked straight in front of me. On the seat opposite was
seated a soldier, the only human presence in the whole
garden. I concentrated my attention upon the soldier.

I then became aware that, between the soldier and the
trees, the seat, the gravel, the fountain, the bushes and in
fact all the objects surrounding him, a kind of competition,
or rather, to be more precise, a contest, was in progress. The
soldier, in a subdued, resigned, indifferent voice, sent me
this piece of information: "I am a soldier." But all the
other objects round him, on the other hand, were asserting

115

their identity with voices that were far more peremptory, as much as to say: "There's no one here but me. The others don't exist."

Moreover in the actual figure of the soldier there were certain details which showed that they had a vitality greater than his own. His boots, for instance. "We are boots," proclaimed the two black objects clumsily placed on the white gravel, one this way and one that; "perhaps you may not have realized it, but we are nothing less than boots." Disconcerted by such self-complacency, and after considering his two pieces of footwear for a little, I raised my eyes to the soldier himself who was sitting bent over, his elbows resting on his knees, deciphering, as far as I could make out, a strip cartoon magazine. I had not been mistaken; there was truly a contest between the soldier and the objects that surrounded him. Now, in fact, the absorbed face of the young man no longer said to me: "I am a soldier"; but, like a postulant producing a certificate of education or a title of nobility or a decoration in order to be listened to, it asserted, with a kind of tentative, secretly discouraged emphasis: "I am a man." I lowered my eyes again. A piece of waste paper on the ground beside the seat screamed at me, with feckless violence: "I am a piece of waste paper." How far more sure of itself, more real and, in its way, more profound was this piece of paper than the dull, expressionless face of the soldier.

I felt almost suffocated, and all the more so because an idea had come into my head: supposing my wife were right? Supposing she were really, for me, just a thing like any other thing, neither more important nor more significant than other things? I got up and started off homewards, almost at a run; I entered the building and opened the door of the flat. Disregarding the large number of objects

116

which called out to me in the dim light to make me aware of their presence, I went straight to the bedroom. I knew that my wife must be there.

The door was ajar; I opened it slightly and stood there looking round. The white curtains at the windows kept the room in an even light, neither too strong nor too feeble; the objects in the room might be said to have neither shadows nor degrees of light and shade; their volume, their colours, their lines were clear, pure, precise but without inequalities of tone or relief : all these objects in the bed-room were, democratically, equal, not one of them was, or looked, more visible, more significant, more expressive than another. The vase of flowers on the chest-of-drawers was equal to the carafe of water on the bedside table; the lamp beside the bed was equal to the armchair at the window; the wardrobe was equal to the dressing-table. My eye ranged over all these things seeking a pretext, a reason for preference. No, there was nothing. My wife's head, en-closed and hidden in the hollow of her arm, was equal to the pillow in which it was sunk; her body, to the coverlet on which it was curled up; her feet, to the silk quilt upon which they rested. I looked intently at the huddled body; certainly my wife was weeping because I heard a moan-ing sound mingled with sighs and subdued murmurs, but this sound seemed to me no more interesting or important than the sound made by the transistor on the chest-of-drawers which, turned down low, was humming stealthily. Then, from my wife's whole person, there came a clear, peremptory message : "What are you doing, looking at me? Get it into your head, once and for all, I'm a thing just like other things, nothing more than a thing." So then I closed the door again, very gently, and went away on tiptoe.

# Ambiguities

The traffic lights were red, a fine ruby red; but I, although I saw that they were red, in some way or other merely noticed that they were red and drove on. The blast of a whistle halted me abruptly; and then the constable, slow, ritualistic, self-satisfied, sadistic, raised his arm and beckoned to me to draw up beside the pavement. I obeyed. The constable came over to me, still with the same slowness, slipping off his big black leather gloves; he leant against the door of the car. "So the red light," he said, "means nothing to you?"

I was struck by his turn of expression. He had not asked me, as one might reasonably have expected : "Didn't you see that the light was red?" but rather : "The red light means nothing to you?" Thus, by a simple exchange of verbs, the subject of the sentence was no longer myself, the absent-minded driver, but the traffic light which at that moment, by its redness, was actually saying something to me. "I'm sorry," I stammered, "I was absent-minded."

There are two classes of policemen. There are those who impose the penalty in silence; and those who, on the other hand, not merely impose the penalty but deliver a sermon. This one belonged to the second class. "Ah, so you're absent-minded," he said. "But if, let us say, you were in the company of a beautiful lady, I bet you'd pay careful attention to the look in the lady's eyes. You certainly wouldn't mistake a kind for an unkind look. Well, my dear sir, the

118

traffic light is a beautiful woman. One must pay attention to her glances and understand when she says: stop, it's not the moment; and when she says: all right, go on, it's your turn. Absent-minded, eh? And now please show me your driving-licence and car licence. The fine is one thousand lire."

I didn't say a word; I showed him the documents, paid the fine and drove off. But something had happened to make me realize now that I did not so much look at objects in order to observe them and note their various aspects, as study to put myself in a receptive state of mind, in such a way as to be able to receive their signals, their indications, their messages, in fact. Before the fine imposed upon me, I would see the objects and, when necessary, try to understand them; but they would remain as they were, before my eyes, inert, lifeless, silent. Now, on the other hand, the objects were alive, extremely alive, more alive than I, even though it was with an ambiguous, equivocal, not very candid kind of life. They were all saying something; but, since they said a great many things at the same time, it was very difficult to understand what they were really saying. To give an example (and this thought consoled me a little for the fine), the traffic light just now had said at least three things: (1) I am red; (2) I am a thing of metal and glass and I call myself a traffic light; (3) Stop, otherwise you are breaking the rules of the road. Not to mention that it might also have said: I am an annoyance that is not necessary. I am an arbitrary power against which you ought to rebel. And so on. No need to specify which of all these messages was the one that concerned me.

Well, I drove on and very soon arrived at the ugly building in which Gisella lived, in Corso Vittorio. The entrance-hall was dark, the lift rickety and smelly, the landing plunged in gloom (all of these were signals, indications, messages, each one more urgent than the other; but I was in a hurry and did not bother to take them in). I rang the bell, waited anxiously; a minute, perhaps, went past, and then I could not help, this time, interpreting the message which the old door with its big embossments gave me, shouted at me in fact, with all its strength: "There's nobody there, it's no use waiting, you'd better go away." But evidently I was mistaken and the message was different; for finally the door was opened and Gisella stood on the threshold.

"Oh, Luigi," she exclaimed at once, "how punctual you are! In fact you're actually early. I was expecting you at seven and it's only half past six. But it's nice to see you, just the same. Come in, come in!"

I became conscious that even words, in my new manner of looking at things, did not signify what they seemed to signify. Gisella's words, for example, sent me the following message, or at least so it appeared to me: "Idiot, what on earth d'you mean by appearing half an hour before the time and catching me unprepared and not yet dressed?"

Gisella was, in fact, in her dressing-gown; and her young, rather fragile body, with its wide hips and narrow shoulders, its long neck and small head, like that of a little dinosaur, moved in a heavy, sleepy, lazy way amongst her peach-coloured draperies as she preceded me down the shadowy passage towards the sitting-room. She went in, turned abruptly to me and said: "Now you must wait for me, I've still got to get dressed," and then disappeared.

Feeling uneasy, I walked over to the window, rested my forehead against the glass and looked out. On the front of the building opposite could be seen the luminous sign of a brand of automobiles (again a message); and below the cornice, the lighted windows of an office, with typists sitting at desks and men coming and going about the room dictating to them (another message). I went on looking for a little, then turned back suddenly into the room, as though to take the objects there by surprise and not allow them the time to recover and lie to me.

I noticed as usual that the objects, for the most part, sent out more than one message, some of them two, some of them four, some half a dozen. For instance, the big sofa-bed which occupied one whole wall said four things to me. First of all : I am covered with old patterned uphol-stery, rather dirty on the arms and the back; in the second place : I am a sofa-bed and at night someone who is not Gisella sleeps on me; in the third place : my cushions are disarranged and reveal the pressure of two bodies which were sitting on them recently; in the fourth place : Gisella has no money, otherwise she would have already taken steps to replace my shameful covering. A man's red sweater thrown over the arm of the sofa-bed, on the other hand, said only two things : I am red; I belong to somebody who took me off a short time ago. Finally there were objects which said only one thing : "I am a vase with the roses you sent yesterday to Gisella." "We are two cigarettes still burning." "I am a woman's handkerchief which has fallen on the carpet at the foot of the bed." I realized that there was not a single, silent object, no object that failed to trans-mit a message. They all spoke, all of them. And they were all ambiguous and sinister, all had more than one meaning.

I went over to an open drawer and the first message I received came from a bill and a letter attached to it from a dressmaker demanding payment in peremptory terms. The

121

message which the bill and the letter conveyed to me seemed to me to be perfectly clear: "We are a bill and a letter asking for payment of the bill. We are here to tell you that Gisella wishes to be smart and well-dressed but does not pay. Yet somebody will have to pay, don't you think?"

I did not have time to reflect upon this message, which in any case was extremely explicit, before I received another one, full in the face, immediately afterwards. It was transmitted from one of those reddish-yellow envelopes in which photographers put photographs after developing them. The envelope was open, the photographs scattered about. The message went like this: "We are photographs of a dark young man of about thirty; Gisella took us during a trip into the country. What d'you say to that?"

I turned towards a bookshelf and at once received two more messages: "We are a dozen detective stories, the only reading of Gisella, an ignorant, uncultivated woman." "I am the photograph of Gisella's late husband. But is it really true that he's dead?" There was a looking-glass near the door, and I went up to it to adjust the knot of my tie— a gesture which, in me, denotes perplexity and uneasiness. And this was the message of the looking-glass: "You're fifty. What are you doing here, in the home of this enigmatic woman, who is probably of doubtful character? What are you waiting for? Why don't you go away?"

I did not wait to be told twice. I went out on tiptoe, ran down the stairs two at a time, ran to my car which I had left in a side street, jumped in and drove off as fast as I could. Shortly afterwards, the sudden blast of a whistle brought me to an abrupt halt on the far side of a traffic-light which, alas, showed red. A policeman, as usual slow, self-satisfied, ritualistic, sadistic, came over to me and leant

122

against the door of the car. "To you, I suppose, red and green are the same thing?"

He imposed the usual fine. I watched him while, with bent head, he scribbled in his notebook, and I could not help receiving a message from his left cheek: "I am the constable's left cheek. He did not shave this morning. He has a fine big boil close to his nose, into the bargain." The man's voice, impatient, gave me a start. "You certainly are absent-minded, aren't you? Come on, let me have the thousand lire."

Later, as I was driving along the crowded street, I recalled the policeman's remark: "To you, I suppose, red and green are the same thing"; and then I wondered whether possibly I had not been mistaken when I received the messages from the objects in Gisella's flat. Perhaps I had not understood properly; perhaps Gisella was not in need of money, was really a widow, and had nothing more than a friendship with the dark young man of the photographs; perhaps, above all, in view of their obvious malice, the objects had lied to me, saying one thing instead of another, with the sole purpose of making fun of me. I sighed, then started off in the direction of the country. I was in need of pure air, feeling myself choked by doubt and indecision.

I drove for about twenty minutes along the Via Cassia and then it seemed to me that the trees, the sky, the meadows, the hills, the woods and the farm-houses were all conveying one single message to me, which went more or less like this: "We are here, ready to make a setting for you when you drive out in this direction with Gisella. Why do you hesitate to do this?"

To put it briefly, I turned back and, at the first petrol station, I stopped, got out and telephoned to Gisella. I

123

heard her voice at the other end of the wire saying : "But what happened? Why did you run away? I was so upset." I told her some sort of a lie, assured her that I was hurrying back, invited her to dinner. And then, as I was driving back to Rome, I tried to interpret the message contained in Gisella's words, but this time I was unsuccessful.

# Words are Sheep

It is said that we say what we think, or what we think of saying in substitution for what we think. It is said that we choose words to say what we say. It is said that in the first place it is we who wish to communicate, and then come the words that we use to obtain communication. This may even be true. But it may also be that we speak words which do not in any way concern us; that it is not we who choose the words but the words which choose us; and that, finally, it is the words that are there first, completely ready in advance, and then we make use of them.

Here is proof of it. Yesterday I went to see Gino, a painter friend of mine who lives in Trastevere. The reason for the visit was not the usual one that might be imagined in such a case—the painter's pictures. The reason was a different one : Gino had robbed me of my girl friend, Ginetta; and I was going to see him in order to confront him and perhaps even to assert my rights by means of my fists. My programme was clear-cut; and I wish it to be noted that, in order to put this perfectly clear-cut programme into effect, I had even prepared the remark with which I should open the conversation : "Gino, yesterday evening something was reported to me which made me feel it necessary to come and see you today and ask you for an explanation." Rather a clumsy, complicated remark, if you like; but one that faithfully reflected my state of mind and the character of my relations with Gino.

125

So I climbed up four floors of an ancient, narrow staircase in a tumbledown old house at the end of an alley, reached his door and rang the bell. Gino, in a thick sweater, tight trousers and shammy-leather slippers, opened the door and welcomed me with well-acted delight : "Why, Mario, so it's you! Come in, Mario, I was just thinking of you; come along, I want to show you my latest pictures."

I realized I must speak quickly, before he, with his feigned cordiality, succeeded in weakening my determination. I coughed, then began : "Gino, yesterday evening . . ."

I have already observed that the remark I had prepared was clumsy and complicated; but after all it was just what I had to say. Instead, to my astonishment, I realized that, after this preamble : "Gino, yesterday evening . . .", other words which I did not wish to say and which had nothing at all to do with my relations with Gino started coming out of my mouth, words that were logical and coherent and like sheep which, if the leader of the flock throws itself into a ravine, all throw themselves after it, deaf to the cries of the shepherd. Here is the entire sentence, that is, the flock of sheep, as it came out of my mouth : "Gino, yesterday evening we were at the usual restaurant, Giorgio, Clara, Ginetta and I; but you didn't come. We waited for you and then finally left a note at the desk and went off to the cinema. What were you doing, I should like to know?"

I was amazed. So I myself had not spoken; the words had spoken for me. I had said : "Yesterday evening . . ." and that had sufficed : all the rest had come out by itself. Gino, in the meantime, had gone over to a table and had rapidly squeezed out various tubes of paint on to his palette. Then he went and stood in front of a big canvas lit from below by a powerful lamp. "D'you mind if I go on working, Mario?" he asked. "What was I doing yesterday evening? Nothing, I stayed at work in the studio."

He turned his back on me and diligently retouched one corner of the picture with his brush. I thought that perhaps it would be a good plan if I made him understand my state of mind indirectly, by means of some hostile, disagreeable remark. For instance, by speaking ill of his pictures, which hitherto I had always praised. Occasionally I write art criticism, and two years before I had written the introduction to an exhibition of Gino's. An opinion of mine expressed in this way: "For some time now, Gino, your pictures have been getting worse and worse," could not fail to vex him. Thus, what with his vexation and my resentment, an argument would be started and the truth about Ginetta would come out somehow or other. So I opened my mouth and announced: "Your pictures, Gino..."

The power of words. The simple but unusual remark (for who after all goes and tells a painter that his pictures are bad?) was replaced, on the tip of my tongue, so to speak, by a remark more complicated but usual, at any rate in the language of present-day art criticism: "Your pictures, Gino, have for some time been clearly displaying a different method of composition. You have been able to free yourself from last year's work-hypotheses and transfer to a decidedly anti-humanistic plane, with a resoluteness that bears all the signs of a contest . . ." Once again I was amazed, as I took stock of the verbal sheep, bleating but disciplined, as they issued from my mouth and hurtled into the void. He did not turn round but, still continuing with his painting, observed in a friendly way: "The things you say, Mario, are very good and very just. Why don't you do the introduction for my next show and include in it the very nice things you've just said?"

127

I could have bitten my hands with rage. I reflected that it was of no use for me to prepare sentences, since there was always another sentence, much more logical and natural even if absurd, to replace them on my lips at the last moment. I said to myself that I would utter any word that came into my head, without worrying about the others which it might drag along behind it. I said, suddenly: "Today . . ."

Today, what? "Today" was a word laden with implications: it might drag in its wake any sort of a sentence, possibly even one that concerned Ginetta, such as, for example: "Today, however, I came to see you in order to bash in your face . . ."

But not at all. This particular "today" had nothing to do with Ginetta. It was a very special "today", a "today" which was followed by its own little flock of sheep and had no intention of getting rid of them. It was a "today", in fact, entirely independent, as usual, of my will. What I said was: "Today, Gino, as soon as I leave here I want to go and buy myself a pair of soft-leather slippers like yours. Can you tell me where you found them?"

He raised his arm to adjust the light of the lamp on his picture as he answered me: "I bought them at Porta Portese. They're black market things, English. Nice, aren't they?"

He went on painting; and then I came to grips with my problem, I put it with its back to the wall, so to speak. I *had* to speak to him about himself and Ginetta. Therefore I must start the conversation with a word that could only refer to him and Ginetta. And what word could be better fitted to attain this end than his own name? I began resolutely: "Gino . . ."

"Well, what is it?"

128

"Gino . . ."

"Well, what d'you want?"

"Gino . . ."

Once again I was astonished. I had in fact hit upon a word that did not drag any other word along behind it, that was isolated, solitary, unique; a sheep that was separated from the flock, that had gone astray, even though it, too, might be longing to hurl itself into the void. Luckily he, without intending it, came to my rescue. "You go on repeating my name. Perhaps you think it's too common; but it isn't so at all. D'you know what Gino stands for?"

"Aren't you called Gino?"

"Never again. You won't believe it, but my real name is Iginio."

He gave a laugh and went on painting. I lit a cigarette, watched him for a little, deep in thought; then, in great haste, I said: "Gino, there's something I must say to you."

I took a deep breath; I had done it. The phrase was not ambiguous; if sheep there had to be, this time they should be *my* sheep. More dissimulating than ever, he asked: "There's something you must say to me? What is it?"

"Ginetta is one of those women for whom the fact of loving . . ."

I intended to finish like this: ". . . does not, alas, exclude having adventures from time to time with Tom, Dick and Harry. Possibly even with you." But I had not reckoned with the greater force of attraction, like a magnet with steel, of the more usual proposition in respect of the more rare one. What I had intended to say stuck in my throat. What I actually uttered was: ". . . Ginetta is one of those women for whom the fact of loving is a serious thing."

Just the opposite, in fact, of what I had meant to say.

He replied with conviction: "I believe it"; and I, in desperation, rose to my feet. He turned and asked me: "Are you going away?" And I, still in the grip of that accursed logic of words, answered: "Yes, I have things to do; and Ginetta is expecting me to go with her to the cinema."

I saw that he gave me a strange look, as though he had guessed that my words had no relation to reality and were, so to speak, no more than a kind of pun. Ginetta, in fact, was not expecting me and we were not going together to the cinema. But he said nothing and accompanied me to the door.

I went down and, when I was in the street, raised my eyes, almost involuntarily, and looked at Gino's windows. And then, at one of the windows, I saw Ginetta. There was no doubt, it was she; I recognized her, if by nothing else, from her hair lying loose on her shoulders, curly and puffed-out and unrestrained, of a dull, melancholy brown that seemed to make her face look paler, her eyes darker and more profound. It was only for an instant; she withdrew at once, or rather she vanished like a ghost, and I went on my way. So Ginetta was up there in Gino's studio, she had been in the adjoining room all the time while we were talking. But, according to the words I had spoken, she was in some place that I did not know, waiting for me to take her to the cinema. Which was right, the words which indicated that she was far away from Gino's studio, or my eyes which had seen her at the studio window?

# Doubles

One day recently I came to a decision. I picked out an advertisement in which a "good room, sunny, bathroom; friendly atmosphere" was offered at an address a very long way from my own; I got into my car and went there. I live in a turning off the Via Cassia, almost in the country; the room of the advertisement was in a turning off the Via Appia Nuova: so great a distance seemed to me a safe guarantee of independence, secrecy and, above all, dissimilarity.

I myself did not know precisely what I wanted to do. Was I to embark seriously on a double life, with two homes, one near the Via Cassia and one near the Via Appia? I was a student, with my family in the provinces, and it would be easy to make each landlady believe that I had to spend fifteen days out of thirty in the country. Or was I, on the other hand, merely to take a look at the double life, but without—for the moment, anyhow—practising it? To sound out its possibilities, to get the taste of it?

Yes, that was it; because I did not desire a double life with the object of giving vent to some unavowable instinct; I did not aspire, let us say, to be a faithful fiancé on the Via Cassia and a Don Juan on the Via Appia. No, I had nothing to hide or to give vent to in secret; I merely wished to duplicate myself, that is, to become two people instead of one—and indeed by doing the most innocent and normal

131

things. The double life, in fact, was for me not a means but an end.

I found the house of the advertisement in a turning off the Via Appia that very much resembled the street in which I lived near the Via Cassia: two rows of modern buildings, the surface of the road uneven and full of holes and hummocks and, at the far end, a strip of blue sky above a strip of green countryside. Moreover the building itself was like the one in which I lived: the same eight-storey façade riddled with windows and balconies, the same marble entrance-hall, the same lift-shaft, the same staircase, the same balustrade. I reflected that this, after all, was not so very strange: the building had probably been constructed with the same materials, at the same period, perhaps even by the same firm and according to the plans of the same engineer. I reached the fourth floor. I could hardly believe my eyes when I saw that the nameplate bore the name of my Via Cassia landlady: "Longo". Then I reflected that this was not an entirely improbable coincidence: Longo was not an uncommon name; in the telephone directory there was a page and a half of Longos. I rang the bell.

As I waited I was conscious of the same secret feeling of expectation that I had experienced when I rang at the door of Signora Longo No. 1, near the Via Cassia. Moreover this feeling of expectation had not been falsified, for the door had been opened by the lady's daughter, Elena, with whom I had lost no time in forming a mildly amorous relationship. And now the door opened and a gentle voice said: "Yes, what is it?"

I looked up. Elena was fair, this one was dark; Elena's face bore all the signs of health, with its blue eyes, pink cheeks and scarlet mouth; this girl, on the other hand, had a delicate, pale, almost wasted face with two enormous dark, shining eyes. But the welcome was the same: discreet, reticent, even shy, but not indifferent—the usual welcome of a girl who finds herself confronted by a young man of her own age.

I explained what I wanted. She at once showed me into the sitting-room, announced that she would go and tell her mother, and disappeared. I looked round: in the home of Signora Longo No. 1 the predominant style was sham Renaissance; here it was sham Louis XVI; but I felt that this dissimilarity was only apparent and that, like the two Longo daughters, these two styles of decoration had, as far as concerned me, the same "intention". What this "intention" might be, I could not have said; but that it was the same, I was certain. I sat down and then almost shuddered as I recalled that Elena, too, had said, that day: "I'll go and tell Mother."

Soon the mother appeared. The same phenomenon was again repeated with regard to her as had formerly occurred in the case of Signora Longo No. 1: I did not see her. I was indeed aware that I had in front of me something mellifluous, homely, provincial, calculating and authoritative; but I failed to see what kind of a face and figure Signora Longo No. 2 had, just as, even now, I did not know what Signora Longo No. 1 looked like. Of course we all know that there are people who may even have an intense, though concealed, life, but who nevertheless make no more effect than a damp stain on a wall.

Anyhow, the following dialogue took place between us. "You are a student?"

"Yes, I'm studying literature."

"And your family, where are they?"

"At Ancona."

"A fine city, Ancona. I have a cousin at Ancona. Are you an only son?"

"Yes."

"I'm afraid you must be terribly spoilt, then. You only children . . . For example, my Elena . . ."

I gave a start. "Who is Elena?"

"My daughter."

"Excuse me. You were saying?"

"Ah yes, I was saying that, alas, Elena too is an only child."

"Why alas?"

"I should have liked so much to have a son. I always let the room to young men like you. Then I can partly deceive myself into thinking I have a son."

"I knew that too"; the remark escaped me.

"What?"

"I knew that you wanted so much to have a son and, not having one, that you let the room to young men like me."

"Excuse me, but how did you come to know that?"

"Well, I guessed it, when you told me that Elena is an only daughter and when I saw you sigh."

"You're very intuitive, there's no denying it. Anyhow, don't worry: here you'll be like one of the family, but at the same time you'll be free, perfectly free. Would you like to see the room?"

"Thank you, yes."

We went out into the passage; there was a door open, and at the far end of a long, narrow room, facing the window, Elena No. 2 was sitting at her desk. Her mother, as we went past, said: "Elena, let me introduce Signor . . . What is your name? Excuse me."

"Fabiani."

134

"Signor Fabiani, who is very soon coming to stay with us here."

Elena jumped up and at once came towards us, as though she were merely waiting to be called. We shook hands, and I noticed that, during my conversation with her mother, Elena had changed her clothes. When she had opened the door to me, she had been wearing a little green dress, rather shabby; now she had put on a red blouse and a grey skirt, both of which looked new. She followed us, and we went into the room, all three of us.

"The room is both light and quiet; on fine days you can see the Castelli Romani; this is the bathroom; all the furniture is new; this way, by this door, you can go in and out without anyone noticing." Signora Longo No. 2 went backwards and forwards, opening the windows, displaying drawers and cupboards, exactly as Signora Longo No. 1 had formerly done. And, as then, Elena stood aside looking at us; and I, instead of looking at the furniture and the landscape, looked at Elena. Then the repeated ringing of the telephone-bell was heard, and her mother said she was going to answer it and went out, leaving us alone.

I was standing near the door; Elena was at the other end of the room, near the window. We looked at one another, exactly as, in analogous circumstances (but that time it had been the front door bell) in the Longo No. 1 home, I and the other Elena had looked at one another. And in that moment, as with the other Elena, I realized that the girl was begging me to take the room and that I was promising her that I would do so. I felt that I had fallen on my feet; or rather that, just as the materials used, the plan adopted, the engineer and the firm entrusted with the job had brought it about that the building in which I found myself at the moment was in every respect

135

similar to the one in which I lived near the Via Cassia; so, in the same way, an incommensurable number of forces was bringing it about that I should behave with Elena No. 2 in precisely the same way as I had behaved with Elena No. 1. Then, suddenly, an idea occurred to me: *this* was the double life, not that entirely different life that I had pictured. A life, that is, whose principal quality was not so much to change by changing its place and its circumstances, as to remain substantially identical. The feeling of duplication at which I had aimed was, fundamentally, just this: to acquire the consciousness, in doing something, that I had done it already and that anyhow it was impossible for me not to do it in precisely that way and no other.

This reflection lasted no more than a second. Then Signora Longo came back into the room, saying: "Wrong number."

There was nothing left for me but to go away. I told Signora Longo that I would give her my answer next day, I shook hands with Elena who left her hand in mine perhaps a moment longer than was necessary (as the other Elena had done); then I went down to the ground floor in the lift that was so like the one in the building near Via Cassia, even to the rude words scrawled on the glossy wood with the point of a nail.

I returned home. Scarcely had I thrown myself down on my bed, tired after so many adventures, when there was a knock at my door and Elena's voice said: "Telephone."

As I went out to take the call, Elena followed me and, while I was telephoning, took my hand and played with my fingers. At the other end of the line I heard the voice of the other Elena say: "Signor Fabiani?"

"Yes?"

"My mother asks me to tell you that there's no need for

136

you to give her an answer. There was someone under consideration before you, and my mother has decided to let this other person have the room."

I enquired at once, hurriedly: "Who is this someone?"

"A student called Mariani."

"Ah, a student. And what's he like? Dark, fair, tall, short —what's he like?"

"You're rather strange, aren't you? He's more or less like you, neither dark nor fair, neither tall nor short, so-so. But why d'you want to know?"

"Thank you, I'm sorry, good-bye." I hung up the receiver: Elena came close to me and said in a whisper: "Who was that woman? What is there between you and her?"

I should have liked to reply: "That woman was you. Between me and her there is exactly what there is between you and me. Or rather, the student Mariani, who is so like me, does with her what I should have been able to do, and so there's no need for me to take the room off the Via Appia since he will see to doing everything for me. And all of us, if we want to, can live not merely two lives at the same time but millions; all that's necessary is for us to be aware that we're identical with millions of other people in the world." But I thought she would not understand me and so I answered her with a lie of some kind and went back to my room and threw myself down on the bed again. It occurred to me that at that very moment an infinite number of other people like me were throwing themselves on their beds and, strange to say, this thought comforted me, and, still thinking that I was doing something that so many others were doing, I fell asleep.

# A Disengaged Conscience

I have a bad memory and there's nothing to be done about it. I forget everything: the day, the time, names, numbers, people's faces, events, engagements. But whereas with some people forgetfulness comes from having, as they say, other things in one's head, I myself have nothing at all in my head. Or rather, I ought to have the things which I forget; but since I forget them, I have nothing.

My wife says that I forget because, in my unconscious, I wish to forget. This is a modern and up-to-date way of telling me that I am timid and that I don't like facing reality. She also says that I forget because I have no sense of time and that I have no sense of time because I do not work and therefore have nothing in my life that makes progress, that develops, that has any result. It may be so. But what fault is it of mine if she is rich and wanted to marry me and thus helped me to become forgetful, eccentric, futile?

I have tried various things to combat my forgetfulness. Among other things, I write down in a note-book, every morning, all the orders and appointments for the day. But, since I often forget to go and look in the note-book, my wife, who never forgets anything, takes it upon herself to remind me, at the moment when I am going out, of the things that I have to do. And so it was today. She entered like a fury when I was still lying on the bed for my afternoon rest and, leaning against the bed-head, cried to me: "Wake

138

up! D'you want me to read out what you have to do this afternoon?"

"Yes, do."

"Go to the chemist, buy toothpaste, pick up the theatre tickets, look at page 561, volume 1, encyclopedia."

I opened my eyes wide in astonishment. "What does that mean, what has the encyclopedia to do with it?"

"How should I know? It was you who wrote it down, so you must know what it means. Well, good-bye, I'm off."

"Why, where are you going?"

"I've a whole lot of things to do; I'm an active person, I am. See you this evening, good-bye."

I reflected a little longer on the strangeness of the sibylline note I had made, then I got up, put on a dressing-gown and went into the sitting-room. I took down the first volume of the encyclopedia from the shelf, and there indeed, at the top of page 561, was the note: "Go to Via Solferino, number 64."

For some time I stood lost in astonishment, looking at those words written by my own hand and yet, to me, incomprehensible. Why, in the first place, had I not written them straight into my notebook? And then, why in the encyclopedia, of all places? And what was there at that address which required such precautions? Finally common sense suggested to me that only an investigation on the spot in Via Solferino would perhaps be able to provide an explanation of the enigma. So I dressed and went out.

Between the station and the Macao barracks lies one of the dullest, the dreariest, the most decayed quarters of Rome. Built in the time of Umberto I, its streets bear the names of the Risorgimento battles; there one breathes the same atmosphere as in the pages of elementary-school history books. As I turned into Via Solferino, my curious eyes were met by a street typical of that gloomy quarter : long, narrow, flanked by yellowish buildings, dusty, austere, and with rows of regular windows and big entrance-doors. An ideal street, I thought immediately, for anyone who wished to hide, to camouflage himself, to disappear.

Driving slowly, I came to No. 64. First surprise : it was a shop with its shutter lowered. What did this mean?

I stopped, I examined the shutter. It was of the commonest and coarsest kind, of corrugated metal painted grey and rusty in places. As I said, it was lowered, and this detail produced my first piquant reflection : how odd that it should be shut, for it was five o'clock, a time at which all shops were open. I looked again and, as happens in that game which consists in finding the errors in a drawing, I discovered other singularities : above the shutter there was no shop-sign but a long, narrow window, about half a yard high and three yards wide. Furthermore, the lock had been removed and through the hole, instead of the polished surface of the glass door of a shop, could be seen nothing but the rough surface of a wall. This meant that the shop door had been walled up and that the shutter pulled down over the wall fulfilled the same function as a mask over a face. But what did this simulated shop conceal? Probably, I thought, an inhabited room which received its light from the window above the shutter. And how did one get into this room? Equally probably, by the little adjoining door, a door of light varnished wood with a lock and handles of shining brass which, only a step from the old, ugly shutter, revealed, by its brand-new appearance, the recent transformation of the shop into an apartment. And so, in a nutshell, this must be an apartment to be used as a hiding-place, as a secret retreat, the kind of place that is commonly, and deplorably, known as a *garçonnière*. But here my explanation came to a stop. How did I myself come into all this?

Perplexed, deep in thought, worried even, I returned home and went straight into the sitting-room. The encyclopedia was there in its place on the shelf. I pulled out the first volume, turned to page 561, and saw that there were only three items on that page : Adularia, a variety of orthoclastic feldspar which takes its name from Mount Adula (Grisons); Aduli, the ancient seaport of the kingdom of Aksum; Adultery (Latin *adulterium*, from *adulter*, etc., etc.)

It was immediately clear to me that, in writing the address of the apartment in Via Solferino at the top of this particular page, I had meant to allude to one of these three items. Since there was no question of my having wished to refer to "Adularia" or "Aduli", I was forced to believe that the allusion concerned "Adultery". Moreover the very character, disguised and unusual as it was, of the apartment in Via Solferino confirmed this hypothesis. Evidently I had wished in some way to remind myself that this address was connected with the idea of adultery; and I had also wished to remember it without letting my wife know. But whose adultery? There seemed to be no doubt about the answer : my own. I was the adulterer : it was I who had the intention of committing adultery : it was I who was looking for an apartment, to rent or to buy, in which to meet the woman I loved. But how had I come by the address in Via Solferino? And who was the woman?

At this point my suppositions became stranded on the sandbanks of my usual forgetfulness. I thought and thought and came to no sort of conclusion. Memory was a closed door; however much I knocked, it did not open. In the end I was filled with a tremendous vexation : this time I had

141

gone so far as actually to forget the very existence of the woman who, according to all probability, should have a certain importance in my life. Buried in my memory like a treasure in the depths of a cave, I had hidden her so well that I was no longer capable of finding her. All my actions suggested, necessitated her existence; like lava grown cold which retains the imprint of a body, the past revealed her empty shape, but she herself was not there.

I spent a couple of very unhappy hours in this way, between remorse for a betrayal which I do not remember having wished to perpetuate and longing for the figure of a woman which I could not succeed in tracing. I had thrown myself on the bed, and I allowed myself to be submerged in the shadows of twilight. Then I heard sounds, doors opening and shutting, footsteps: my wife had come in again. A little later she appeared in the doorway, a sheet of paper in her hand. "So you believe anonymous letters, do you?" she said.

"What anonymous letters?"

"A vile letter which says that I have meetings with a man, in an apartment in Via Solferino."

I jumped up briskly. "No, my God!" I exclaimed. "I did receive the letter but I did not believe it. The truth is, I had already forgotten I'd received it."

"Nevertheless you kept it."

"Why, where?"

"In a safe place, under a big pot on the terrace. Unfortunately the gardener came and moved the pot; he found the letter and handed it over to me."

"But when did all this happen?"

"About a month ago."

"And so you knew . . ."

"I knew all about it. I also knew that you'd go and

investigate in Via Solferino, as in fact you decided to do today."

So it seemed I had made a note in my notebook of a job to be done, but had taken care to postpone it until a month later, so as to have time to obliterate the cause of it in my memory. And I had hidden the letter in a place that made it almost inevitable that I should forget it. I felt that this time there could be no doubt about it : unconsciously, I had wished to wipe out the remembrance of the whole affair and I had almost succeeded. "Now just imagine," I said, "I had so completely forgotten that letter that today, after having been to Via Solferino, I very nearly came to the conclusion that it was *I* who was intending to be unfaithful to *you*. And so I had a feeling of guilt and I even wondered who the woman was that I wanted to have an affair with."

"Bad conscience," said my wife.

"No conscience at all," I retorted, "either good or bad. If anything, a disengaged conscience."

# The Things that Grow

Everything that grows has for some time interested me, or rather it would be more exact to say that I am obsessed by it. I believe I have made the discovery that the things of the world are divided into two great categories: those that do not move, that do not change, unless someone moves them and changes them; and those, on the other hand, that have a fundamentally monstrous ability to do everything by themselves, even to be born, even to grow, even to die. Metals do not grow, nor stones, nor any of the objects made of metal or stone; plants, on the other hand, grow, as do animals and men. And not only do they grow but, through nourishment, they transform themselves with ease one into another: plant into animal, animal into plant, both into man and man into both of them. I know quite well that this is life, as they say; this does not alter the fact that, while we can be sure that things of stone and metal do not change and therefore the relationship that we have with them does not change either, what can happen between us and plants, between us and animals, between us and men is, to say the least, disquieting. Buy a little unimportant plant and after some time it will cover your house with foliage, and if you don't take care it will even come into the rooms; take a fancy to a pretty little puppy and before a year is out you will have a great big mongrel jumping all over you; get married and . . .

These reflections occurred to me for the first time a few evenings ago, while my wife was dishing out the soup to me and our five children. A habitual gesture that she has been performing for fifteen years; and the china plates with their little flowers and garlands, the white-metal spoons and forks, the tumblers of cheap glass are the same that we had fifteen years ago; just as the brass lamp hanging above the table with its globes and brackets is the same, and so is the table itself, a round, walnut table carved in a sham fifteenth-century style. But in contrast to all these objects made of unchanging, stable materials which have remained as they were fifteen or more years ago, I became aware of a family very different from the one which in the past gathered twice a day in that same room. This discovery came to me as a shock, as to a man blind from birth who suddenly sees. All of a sudden I thought: "Why, what has happened? Who is it that has changed my children and my wife in this way? Who has replaced the pretty young woman I married with this stout, shapeless matron? And my curly-headed babies with these graceless adolescents, covered with hairs and pimples? Who has played this nasty joke on me? And what have I in common with these six people?"

With these thoughts in my head I bent over my plate, filled my spoon, brought it up to my mouth and, as usual, sucked up the soup with my lips, making a slight noise which, to tell the truth, pleases me, and if I don't do this the soup seems to me not so good. My wife at once scolded me sharply. "Don't make that noise sucking up the soup out of your spoon," she said. "It's not only bad manners, but you know it annoys the children."

I looked round to see whether my children were taking my side in face of a remark that was so unkind and was made, into the bargain, in so rude a tone of voice. But no, on the contrary: Gina and Livia took the attitude

145

of elegant young ladies disgusted by their father's coarseness; as for the three boys, Giuliano aged fourteen, Luciano fifteen and Massimiliano sixteen, they were actually making fun of me. They were laughing derisively, in mock protest: "No, no, Mummy, no one's ever said anything. We *like* that noise that Dad makes when he's eating; look, we'll do it too;" and they filled their spoons again and sucked up the soup with a loud noise, copying me. I said to my wife: "That's enough. I won't tolerate remarks about what I do or don't do. Above all I won't tolerate being made fun of by my children at your instigation."

She answered with the calm of one who is convinced of being in the right: "Your children wouldn't make fun of you if you had better manners."

"I do what I like in my own house."

"No, nobody does what he likes. We must all have consideration for others."

I looked round again. My two silly daughters looked more uncomfortable than ever. And the boys were laughing at me again. "We quite understand," they repeated. "Each person must do as he likes." And one of them was scratching his head violently with both hands; another was picking his nose; and the third was ostentatiously cleaning his teeth. "You see," said my wife, "you see what would happen if everyone did as he liked."

Furious but controlled, I took off my glasses and said in a slow, emphatic voice, while pretending to clean the lenses with my napkin: "Ten years ago a very different family was sitting round this same table: a father who was happy because he was loved and respected, a gentle, submissive wife, affectionate children. All that is changed. Evidently something has happened."

"I'll tell you what's happened," interrupted Massimi-

146

liano, the only one of the boys who already shaves although he has only a few ugly hairs here and there on his cheeks and upper lip; "we're no longer children, so we think for ourselves. That's what's happened."

Mentally I compared the Massimiliano of ten years ago with the Massimiliano of today, and I answered with conviction: "No, it's not that you think for yourselves because you're no longer children. You think for yourselves because you're no longer the same."

"Yes, exactly, we're no longer the same because we're no longer children."

Then I looked with hatred at my wife and, pointing my forefinger at her, cried in a voice of thunder: "Who is that shrew, that great fat lump, that hippopotamus? I don't know her. The woman I married was entirely different."

It must be noted that I did not wish to offend my wife, merely to tell her the truth: at that moment I actually had the feeling that one person had been replaced by another. But my words were not understood. My wife stared at me for an instant in amazement; then she took her face between her hands and burst into tears; the girls rushed to her side to comfort her; the boys protested with such violence that I positively feared for my own safety. Then Massimiliano, the most infuriated of the three, cried: "And you—d'you imagine you're not changed too? Have you never looked at yourself in a glass?"

I was disconcerted at having my arguments thus turned back upon myself. "I forbid you to talk like that to your father," I stammered.

"Forbid me or not, I don't care. You have the heart to tell Mummy that she's not like she was once. And how about you?"

Suddenly I felt frightened. "That's enough, that's

147

enough," I cried. "I'm going away. I shan't come back until you've all calmed down."

In the hall, as I was putting on my overcoat, I felt compelled to follow Massimiliano's far from tender advice: I took a hasty glance at myself in the mirror above the console table. The two ebony and bronze caryatids supporting the mirror were still as they had been fifteen years before, black, metallic, funereal. But the face in the glass was sorely changed: yellow, bilious, with two long, deep furrows in the dry cheeks and a confused tangle of grey hair round the forehead. I shook my head angrily, then ran out into the garden and thence into the street.

I live in a little old house in the neighbourhood of Sant' Agnese. It was a damp, mild night, the usual Roman *scirocco* weather; so I went and sat down in a small garden in Via Nomentana in order to calm myself and reflect at leisure. From my bench I could see, on the pavement opposite, the great iron gate, black between its two tall white pillars, of the Villa Torlonia—things, again, of stone and metal, unchanging, as stable today as yesterday, the opposite of my wife, my children and myself. Then I reflected that another characteristic of things that grow and become transformed was the capacity for feeling pain; and I longed to be a stone on the shore instead of a man of flesh and blood capable of suffering and journeying towards unknown and nameless metamorphoses. At that moment I heard someone say: "Why, we've met before!"

I turned and saw beside me on the seat an elderly beggar whom indeed I already knew; but not in the sense he said.

I had already noticed his ragged figure, corpulent and vaguely professorial, on other occasions and in those same gardens, as I went to and from my office. Usually I avoided him; his state of degradation repelled me. But now I felt pity for him, even though I realized that the pity I felt was for myself, like him middle-aged and grey. "Yes, that's true," I said, "but where?"

He was astonished at so unusual a reception. "Where?" he stammered. "I don't know, somewhere or other."

"In another life. In that life I was young and you were young and goodness knows what we did or who we were. In this life here we're no longer young, and you're a beggar and I'm a lawyer. And we don't know one another. Here's something for you; good-bye."

"I don't know what you're talking about, but thanks all the same," he cried after me as I walked away.

I went back and into the garden, and caught a glimpse, in the uncertain light of a headlamp, of the grotesque outline of my wife upright in front of the white marble statue, representing a nymph or a nude goddess, which stands in the middle of a basin on top of a sham rock covered with maiden-hair fern. No doubt she was anxiously awaiting my return. Then I thought: "In another life, of course, after a quarrel like that we should have parted. But in this life, amongst these trees that fifteen years ago were mere bushes, in front of this statue which, on the contrary, has remained as it was, there's nothing left for us but to make peace."

And so it was. But shortly afterwards, as we were sitting together by the basin, looking at the black water in which the white statue was reflected, I could not help thinking aloud: "Ah, what an affliction it is to be human beings, to be born, to grow up, to suffer, to die! I should like to be made of marble, like that statue."

And my wife, already petulant: "Don't think of saying such a strange thing! You already have a heart of stone. It's the heart that counts."

149

# The Monster

After answering the telephone, I went back into my study with the intention of going on reading for another ten minutes or so. Then, according to my custom, I should sleep for half an hour, and after that I should go to my office. But when I looked for the book which I remembered having had in my hand at the moment when my wife called me to the telephone, I could not find it. At first I looked in the obvious places—on the sofa amongst the newspapers and magazines that littered it, on the writing-table, on the chairs; then in the bookcase amongst the books and on top of the books, but it was not there either. I had begun searching calmly and in a leisurely way, then I became irritated and started throwing papers and books about, almost without knowing what I was doing. "Where *is* my book?" I finally shouted. At this cry my wife came in—just as though she had been behind the door; she asked what had happened, then, silent and smiling and elegant in her assured movements, like an all-seeing angel, she climbed on a chair and took down the book from where it was lying, on top of the bookcase, well out of reach. Still without speaking, my wife went away and I was left flabbergasted, book in hand, staring at the bookcase: how had I managed, without being conscious of it, to put the book up there? "I do things without knowing what I'm doing," I said to myself, disconcerted. Then I lay down on the sofa and went to sleep almost at once.

150

I had a dream which nevertheless was not a dream, that is, it was not expressed in images but in a feeling, or linked with a memory. I knew for certain that I had committed a crime, a horrifying, despicable, irreparable, ignominious crime, and I knew also that nobody knew I had committed it, and yet I had a feeling of anguish and fear and above all an atrocious sense of guilt. From this sense of guilt the crime, though entirely undefined in its material circumstances, assumed a character of crushing, peremptory realism: there could be no doubt about it, I had committed a terrible crime. Another curious aspect was that there persisted, side by side with this sense of guilt, a sense of my own innocence which told me that, in spite of the crime, I was still the same Massimo, incapable of doing wrong, and that the crime had been, so to speak, a mere slip or *lapsus*. This sense of innocence likewise explained why I knew nothing about the crime although I was certain of having committed it: obviously the crime had been perpetrated by me in a state of unconsciousness, like someone acting under the influence of drink or drugs.

The crime, or rather the painful memory of the crime, was not represented in my dream, as I have said, by any kind of image, except that of a breathless race through a dark landscape in which there was nothing but shadows, obscure, shapeless presences and nocturnal phantoms. The dream, however, was not silent: a deafening, thunderous, continuous din, like that of a train in a tunnel, accompanied this feeling of rushing through the darkness. At a certain point the din increased, just as the din of a train increases as it draws near the opening of the tunnel; and I awoke.

I immediately thought that my dream, or rather my nightmare, had been caused by something I had eaten, and indeed I recalled that there had been wild boar for

151

lunch and that I had consumed a good quantity of it. I got up and went into the bathroom, where I washed my face and hands, and then, without saying anything to my wife who at that hour was resting, I left the house.

The street in which I live is a short, quiet street: everything that happens in it, a roving dog, the milkman ringing at a door, a couple of children playing, acquires an extraordinary distinctness. As I came out, I at once saw two policemen coming towards me. Immediately my breath failed me, my eyes became dim, my knees gave way beneath me: there could be no doubt of it, the policemen were coming to arrest me for the crime I had committed, that crime without name or shape which was nevertheless so real and which had so precise a character, ignominious, frightful, despicable.

Standing motionless in the doorway, I awaited the policemen. They were of different ages—a young man, dark and thin, and an older man, short and rather stout. It was the latter who spoke: "Are you the owner of this car?"

"Yes."

"You're breaking the law. Your car is parked on a bend."

After that everything went according to the usual formalities. But now my feeling of guilt had been aroused again and it would not leave me. It was real, in the same way that a wound from a blow is real: it was painful and at the same time was a continual reminder of the cause of the pain. To the feeling of guilt was added a curious fixation in time: I had certainly committed the crime three days before, not a day earlier or a day later. One more small effort of memory, I thought with horror as I got into the car and started the engine, one more small effort of memory and the crime would all of a sudden leap o my eyes with precise images of myself, of the victim, of the place, of the actions and the violence and the death.

That small effort, however, I could not manage to make. The crime lay, so to speak, on the tip of my memory—just as one says that a word is on the tip of one's tongue; but, however hard I tried to pull it out, it would not come. Moreover the effort was frustrated by fear; I indeed longed to know what crime I had committed, but at the same time I was afraid of learning it. And indeed, once I knew it, what would become of my life?

My office is a quiet place, favourable to reflection: it is a room shut away at the far end of a corridor, at a film studio, and my work consists in reading scripts and reporting on them to the producer. From my desk I have a view through the uncurtained window of a green, treeless countryside, a view tidily disposed in successive lines of pale, bare hills. I took off the telephone receiver, locked the door, and then, seated in the armchair with my eyes turned towards the window, I started furiously thinking. I was sure that this was not a case of a dream designed to express remorse for a crime of, so to speak, an impersonal, social or atavistic nature; a crime there had certainly been, and it had been I who had committed it, concretely and not symbolically, in objective reality and not in a metaphorical sense. But where and when and in what manner?

First of all I went and looked out the old newspapers which I have a habit of keeping, and I examined the police reports of three days before. There had indeed been a couple of crimes, but in the first place they did not have the ignominious character I was conscious of in the crime I felt I had committed; and in the second place it was already known with certainty who the culprits were. There was

153

nothing left, therefore, but to make a minute reconstruction of that day three days earlier. I lit a cigarette, took a sheet of paper and a pencil, and first of all wrote down the hours, from eight o'clock when I had got up until midnight when I had gone to bed, and then, beside each hour, I noted what I had done. I then discovered a detail which, to say the least of it, was curious : between two o'clock and five in the afternoon there was a gap, three empty hours during which anything might have happened, seeing that I had not the slightest recollection of how I had spent them.

There was, however, one element that might reasonably lead one to suppose that I had committed the crime precisely during those three hours. I was accustomed, if I was not sleeping and if the weather was fine, to go out at once after lunch and drive into the country in the immediate vicinity of the town : I liked this country near the town, arid as it was and pale and impoverished, yet not without valleys and thickets, caves and ravines and winding crevices; I liked to wander through these wild, deserted places, having in sight, all the time, the distant houses of the town, in a white, reassuring line on the horizon. These excursions, however, were not a regular thing; thus I was not at all sure that I had been in the country three days before. But if I had gone there, there could be no doubt about it : I had committed the crime in one of those valleys filled with briars, in which there could often be seen the dark yawning mouths of abandoned quarries or caves of volcanic origin. And what crime was it? It seemed to me clear that, given the place, the hour and the particular nature of my guilty feeling, it must have been a crime of a disinterested kind, so to speak, that is casual, gratuitous, a crime of pure cruelty, in fact a sexual crime. There was no knowing, perhaps I had attacked, raped and killed a woman, pos-

154

ibly a young girl, and had then buried her in one of those caves and had fled; there was no knowing . . .

At this point, anyhow, the investigation came to an end: the crime of which I still retained dread and horror in my memory had no name, and, however great the efforts I made during that afternoon, I could not succeed in finding a name for it. In the end it seemed to me that I was even more frightened at being unable to recall the crime with exactitude than I was at having undoubtedly committed it. And so evening came on. Then I emptied the ashtray, brimming with dead cigarette-ends, into the waste paper basket, opened the window so as to air the smoke-filled room, and went out.

When I reached home I could hear, even from the entrance-hall, the voice of my wife in the sitting-room shouting angrily but in a special tone such as one uses with a child or with someone who does not understand and who one knows does not understand: "Monster, monster, monster! You're a monster; don't come near me, monster that you are, I don't ever wish to see you again, you monster."

It occurred to me suddenly that she was shouting at me, through the door, knowing that I had come in; and once again, as when I had seen the policemen, I had a horrible feeling of dismay. I was, in fact, a monster; only a monster could have committed a crime like mine. My heart in a tumult, I opened the door and entered the room.

My wife was standing in the middle of the room and was shouting at a little Siamese cat which, entirely unconscious of her anger, was rubbing itself against her legs, its tail erect, mewing and raising its lovely blue eyes towards her. "I won't have this cat in the house any more," cried my wife, "it horrifies me."

"But why?"

155

"Its three newly born kittens—d'you know what it did? It ate them, all three of them. It's a horror, I tell you. All it left was the paw of one of them and the tail of another. Go into the kitchen, go and look. And now, just as if there was nothing wrong, it purrs and rubs itself against me and talks to me. Monster, monster, monster."

My wife's tone was not playful; she was truly horrified. "Don't get angry like that," I said. "Cats do these things. Besides, you can't get cross with an animal that doesn't know what it's doing."

"Doesn't know, certainly. But if it at least remembered having eaten them; if at least it was looking for them, if it was crying."

I said all I could to comfort and persuade her, then went and shut myself up in my study. I then recalled the book which I had placed on top of the bookcase a few hours before without being aware of it, and I was more than ever convinced that the crime, if I had really committed it, had also taken place in a similar state of absentmindedness. Moreover the cat, I reflected, had eaten its own children also without remembering it. It was possible, therefore, to act in an automatic manner, without any consciousness of what one was doing; it was possible, therefore, to be a monster without knowing it; was a dream therefore necessary to discover that reality existed and that it was impossible for consciousness not to exist?

# Reconciliation

As soon as I read the advertisement offering the lease of
a furnished flat of five rooms on the fourth floor of a building situated at No. 34 Via dei Villini, I did not stop to
think about it: I left the hotel, got into my car and went
there.

In ten minutes I arrived in Via dei Villini, a turning off
Via Nomentana. The buildings were rather old; there were
iron gates with creepers and oleanders with red or white
flowers. I stopped the car in front of the house in which
I had lived for three years with my wife; I got out and
walked up to the front door at the far end of a small garden
as narrow as a corridor. I pressed the fourth floor bell, and
after a little the door unlocked itself with the familiar buzz-
ing sound. I entered the old hall with its black-and-white
paved floor and started going upstairs, my head bent, my
hand on the banisters.

First floor, second floor, third floor; at the second flight
of stairs after the third landing, I raised my eyes and saw
the feet of the woman who was awaiting me as she stood
on the top step: they were big feet, long, vulgar, and inex-
pressibly cheerful. Continuing my way up the stairs, I enquired: "Is this the flat that's to be let?"

I climbed to the top step and we were face to face; we
looked at one another. She was still the same: green, shining eyes; white, lean face; the mouth very red; and two
soft waves of blonde, puffed-out hair. She hesitated a

moment, just long enough to calculate whether she should accept the play-acting I was proposing; then she said: "Yes, this is it."

"Allow me to introduce myself; my name's Lorini."

"My name's Dora."

"Dora what?"

"Dora Moretti."

This was her maiden name. She led me into the flat, twirled round in the entrance on her lanky, muscular legs and, with a sweeping gesture of her large white hand, said: "The entrance-hall."

"What fine furniture—did you choose it yourself?"

"No, no, I don't know anything about it; it was my husband who chose it."

"You're married?"

"Separated."

She led me down the passage. She was wearing a light green, sleeveless blouse, full and soft, and a short, narrow grey skirt. She opened a door and stood aside, without going in, so as to allow me to pass: "The bedroom."

I had furnished it piece by piece, going round the antique-shops: a Spanish bed with a curly iron back; chairs, wardrobe and wooden chest in the same style. Red curtains at the windows. I noticed an uninhabited look about it; the mattresses were rolled up. "But you don't sleep here?"

"No, I can't bear all these bits of old junk. As I no longer have a servant, I sleep in the maid's room."

I went over to the window, opened it and looked out, as I had been accustomed to do when I lived there, at the great magnolia in the garden next door. She came and stood beside me, lightly touching my arm with hers. "What a lovely garden, isn't it?" she said. "It's not mine but it's just the same as if it was."

158

All of a sudden I asked: "Why did you part from your husband, Signora Moretti?"

She looked at me with a gay light in her eyes: "What a lot of things you want to know! Why d'you want to know that?"

"Ah well, just out of curiosity."

"Well, if you really wish to know: incompatibility of character."

She uttered this formula in a complacent tone that made me smile. "And what exactly do you mean by that?" I insisted.

"I mean that my husband and I were too different: I was a more or less working-class girl; he came of a family in which they were all doctors and professors. I was ignorant; he did nothing but read. I was a lover of dancing and sport and open-air life, of everything that's gay and lively; he was quiet, domesticated, studious, misanthropic, sulky."

"Yes, I see, but sometimes just because people are different . . ."

"And then there was something else."

"What was that?"

"I expected that once we were married he would educate me, would teach me all the fine things he knew. He, on the other hand, expected me to act as cook for him, as housekeeper, as general servant. So in the end we never came together."

"I see. And how did it all end?"

"It ended badly."

She left the window and walked off towards the door, adding: "My husband not only wanted me to act as his servant but also to be convinced that that was all I was good for. D'you know what he used to say to me all day long, like a sort of refrain?"

159

"What?"

"Idiot, you're an idiot, you're pretty but you're an idiot, my idiot that I'm so fond of, my adored idiot."

"Your husband did love you, then?"

"He loved me, I'm not saying he didn't. But to hear yourself called an idiot from morning till night . . ."

She made a vulgar gesture with her hand, as though to indicate an intolerable excess. Then she looked into another room: "My husband's study."

I looked in too. "Oh, what a lot of books! Why in the world didn't your husband take away these, anyhow?"

"I don't know. When he went away, he said he didn't want anything, either furniture or books, that he was leaving me everything. He said that henceforth he would live in an hotel, without furniture and without books."

"What does your husband do?"

"He writes for the newspapers."

"He's a journalist?"

"No, he's not a journalist, he's a critic; he writes critical articles for the paper."

"And you—did you read these articles?"

"No, I didn't read them, he didn't want me to; he said I was an idiot and ignorant and I wouldn't understand. I used to stick them in an album as they were published, that was all I did."

"Did your husband read much?"

"Much? All the time. He used to sit in that armchair there, near the window, and read all day long. He read in bed, too: the book on one side, me on the other."

"But how old is your husband?"

"Not so very old: thirty-six. But it's as though he was ninety. D'you know what he said when I showed myself a bit amorous with him, so to speak?"

"What did he say?"

"Drop that nonsense."

She shut the door again, and opened the adjoining door: "This is the dining-room."

I had furnished this room in the Provençal style. As with the bedroom, I realized at once that she did not use it. "You don't eat here?"

"No, all this dark furniture depresses me. I eat in the kitchen. Besides, this room reminds me of the end of my marriage."

"Why?"

She looked round the room, was silent for a moment and then said slowly: "It was like this. I told you we had no cook, only a maid by the hour. *I* was the cook. I am a very good cook, though I say so myself, and he was determined that I should do the cooking. One morning—it was a Friday—I had made one of my specialities: fish soup *alla livornese*. He was sitting there, at the head of the table, and while he was eating he was as usual reading a book propped up against his glass. At a certain moment, without looking up, he said: 'This fish soup is really exquisite, Dora.' Then I don't know what came over me. I took hold of the tablecloth with both hands and sent the whole of the fish soup flying into his face."

"Really?"

"Yes, really."

"And what then?"

"Then we had an explanation, and the truth came out and I told him I didn't want to live with him any longer, on any conditions, and that I was going back to my parents. At this point he begged me to stay on in the flat, with the furniture, the books and everything else. Then he put a few things into a suitcase and went off to an hotel."

"And have you seen him since?"

"No, it's more than a year now since I've seen him. Sometimes I wonder if he's still the same or if he's changed."

"And what d'you think about that?"

"I think he's still the same. It's not at all easy to change."

"If he's changed, would you take up with him again?"

"Who knows?"

She shut the dining-room door again, went to the end of the passage and opened another small door: "This is the maid's little room. I sleep here now."

It was a room so small that the bed occupied it almost entirely. Her blue muslin nightdress was peeping out from under the pillow; her slippers were on the floor, on the bedside rug; on an armchair there was a towel and on the towel a pair of newly washed stockings. All of a sudden she made an unexpected gesture: she lay down on her back on the bed, her arms raised, her hands under the back of her neck. An impudent gaiety shone in her green eyes. "May I ask you a question, Signor Lorini?"

"Go on."

"Are you married?"

"I'm separated too, like you."

"So much the better. Well then, if you're thinking of taking the flat, I'd like to propose a condition."

"What's that?"

"That you should leave me this little room, the bath-room next door and the use of the kitchen. In exchange I would cook for you, I'd keep the flat in order, I'd take charge, in fact, of all the practical side."

"In other words, you're proposing to act as my servant?"

"If you wish to put it like that—well, yes."

"But haven't you said that you parted from your husband because he wanted you to act as his servant?"

"But you are different from my husband, more understanding, more human, more youthful. With you, I'd willingly act as servant."

She was looking at me, gay and tempting, her arms raised, her hands at the back of her neck. "It's an interesting proposal," I said. "Let's do like this: I'll think it over and give you an answer tomorrow morning."

At that moment there was a ring from the telephone on the bedside table. She took off the receiver and, covering it with her hand, said: "That's understood, then. Do you mind if I don't come to the door with you?"

"Of course not."

I went out. But, when I was already on the stairs, I realized that I had left my hat in the hall. Without giving it any special thought, I turned back, took the key of the flat from my pocket and opened the door. My hat was there, on the table. As I took it, I heard Dora's voice speaking on the telephone: "Cecilia, just fancy who came to see me a few minutes ago . . ."

I listened no farther. I took my hat, went out on tiptoe and noiselessly closed the door.

# The Stammerer

After only two months of matrimony, I began to stammer and, at first, I could not manage to understand why. Later, thinking it over, I discovered the reason for this sudden stuttering: I could no longer succeed in speaking normally with my wife because, at the very moment when I opened my mouth to utter the words, I already felt tired and disgusted with what I was about to say or rather with the way in which I would say it. I had much to say to Fausta, and more every day; but I was repelled by the procedure by means of which, whether more or less consciously, I arranged the words in phrases. This procedure appeared to me to transfer the meaning from the feeling I wished to express to the verbal instrument which I made use of to express it; and, in turn, the instrument seemed to me to be immensely different and remote from the original, and by now inaccessible, feeling. The feeling was like fresh water from a deep spring; the instrument, on the other hand, was—what shall I say?—a mechanism, by which I mean something rigid, metallic, articulated, noisy; something, in fact, resembling a bolt or a spring lock.

Even in the simplest and most direct phrases such as, for instance, "I love you", I was now aware of a clanking of metal, a clattering of machinery, a creaking of joints. I wished to offer Fausta a newly-plucked rose; all I could manage to do, however, was to hand her a verbal nutcracker, totally inexpressive even if perfectly functional.

164

Thus, instead of saying the complete phrase: "I love you", I would start stammering: "I, I, I . . ." Fausta would then come rushing to my assistance: "Speak, speak, what did you want to say to me? Speak!" But indeed, speaking was just what I did not wish to do; because I now felt that, whatever I said, I should still have to say it with a phrase, that is, with a mechanical contrivance.

I therefore took to stammering more and more, especially when I had to express my feeling for my wife. This stammering, moreover, did not displease me: I hoped it would make her think I loved her so much that I was incapable of expressing myself. But in my heart I knew perfectly well that this was not so. Inside my head, indeed, the assembly-line of phrases was all ready to start moving; all that was needed was that I should stop stammering for a moment and soon the succession of phrases would begin coming out of my mouth, unshackled and rational, with its fine nouns and pronouns, its substantives, adjectives, verbs, adverbs and so on.

One summer evening we were sitting, my wife and I, at the kitchen table, for supper. The window was open but all the same it was very hot; Fausta was wearing a little black frock and her arms and shoulders were bare. Then, looking at her, I realized that I had something very important to say to her and that this time I must say it at all costs. The important thing was this: our intimacy was growing and growing every day, but strange to say, the more it grew the more obscure, mysterious and disturbing did our relationship become for me. In other words I was experiencing the opposite of what occurs in the normal experience of life, in which habit generates knowledge, and knowledge indifference. In our relationship, on the contrary, habit was generating ignorance, and ignorance passion. A little far-fetched, perhaps? And not only far-fetched, but extremely fanciful. And yet I felt that behind these painful fancies there was something ineffable (for me, at least) and important, which it was absolutely essential that I should tell Fausta.

Finally I plucked up courage and began: "Fausta, I want to say something to you. Our relationship, for me at any rate, was simpler when . . ." It was some time since I had given utterance to so long a sentence without stammering. Fausta, eager and surprised, at once hastened to encourage me: "When . . . when? . . . Tell me . . . speak!"

"When I . . . I . . ."

"When you . . . what d'you mean? When you loved me less? Or more? When you . . . Finish your sentence, come on, finish it."

"When I . . ."

"Well, say it! When what?"

This time I shook my head and remained silent. She insisted: "But speak, speak! And if you can't manage to speak, at least write it down. Write down what you meant to tell me."

I had a feeling of horror: I was disgusted by *oral* mechanical contrivances, and written ones were even worse. In the end I said: "No, that's enough, I can't say any more."

"But why? Speak, speak!"

"No, it's gone; I've nothing more to say."

"Well, I'm not staying here with you. I'm going into the other room, and when you feel like talking to me, then and only then you can come and find me. Not before." With these words she got up and went out.

I stayed for a short time sitting at the kitchen table; then I got up and wandered round the other rooms, but without having the courage to go into the bedroom, where I knew that Fausta had shut herself up. In the end I went out.

I started walking down a long, dark, tree-lined avenue that lies behind my home. I live in a modern residential quarter with no cafés nor cinemas nor shops, and it was late into the bargain : no one passing. I went on for a little without thinking of anything, more perplexed than worried, with the vague feeling that, by walking in this way, without any purpose, I might hit by chance upon the solution of my problem of expression.

Suddenly, while I was passing along beside a garden gate covered with creepers, I heard the sound of voices. I slackened my step. On the threshold of a little side-gate I caught a glimpse, in the shadows, of two figures, a man and a woman. The male figure was that of a youth in a red sweater and black trousers, the woman could scarcely be seen, hidden as she was by the form of her companion who was pressing against her and standing over her so that he appeared to be urging her to do something. Meanwhile they were talking and I heard the following dialogue :
"Come on !"
　"No."
　"Come on !"
　"No."
　"Why ?"
　"Never mind."
　"Silly !"
　"Leave me alone."
　"Come along !"
　"Stop it !"
　"Good-bye."
　"Good-bye."

I saw that what had happened was this: the young man had asked the girl for a kiss and she had refused him. Then he had called her silly and finally had gone away. I could see him, in fact, walking away beneath the trees of the avenue, whistling to conceal his disappointment. As for the girl, who was probably a servant with her employers away on holiday, she had promptly gone back into the garden, shutting the gate behind her.

But the romance or adventure or story of these two did not interest me. What had struck me, on the other hand, was the manner in which their dialogue had been carried on. Almost entirely in single words, even though these had been uttered with very different intonations; no sentences, that is, no mechanisms, or rather, no intervention of reason. A number of things had happened: request for a kiss, refusal, insult, dismissal; many feelings had flared up and died down: desire, repugnance, hope, scorn, disappointment, anger, resignation; but all had been contained within the limits of the most rigorous irrationality. I, no longer knowing how to communicate with Fausta, had had recourse, instinctively, to stammering. And now these two, the working-class young man and the servant-girl, had given me an indirect lesson.

I went back home and, without turning on any lights, walked through the dark rooms to the bedroom. Fausta was there, curled up in bed but awake, apparently deep in thought. Without stammering, I said. "I've a proposal to make to you."

"What's that?"

"Let's talk to each other for a bit in single words only, without any sentences, in exclamations."

I saw her melancholy black eyes light up with a childish gaiety, as though my proposal had brought to the surface,

168

beneath the woman she now was, the little girl she had once been. Nevertheless she said: "I don't understand."

I explained, still without stammering. She began laughing and laughed for quite a long time. Then she threw her legs outside the bed, stood up and said: "All right, I agree. We'll see whether you stammer less. Let's begin at once, shall we? But you must run after me."

"Why?"

"Because if I run it'll come easier to me. Come on, I'll run away and you'll chase me." As she said this she ran off out of the room, crying: "Run!"

"Wait!"

"Cuckoo!"

"Stop!"

"Here!"

"Tell me!"

"What!"

"Nothing."

"Run!"

"Wait!"

Since that night we always talk like that, Fausta and I. As for long, articulated, well-arranged phrases, I keep them in reserve for the office, for shops, for business matters, in fact for the practical occasions of life. And, by the way, I don't stammer any more.

# Man of Power

He was sitting opposite me, behind the big desk—as much as twelve feet long, perhaps—of antique carved walnut. The room was immense, with red damask on the walls and a frescoed, vaulted ceiling. There was no other furniture in it except his desk, his armchair and my chair. I looked at him: he was wearing a dark suit, with a dark tie and a white shirt; he gave the impression of a soldier in civilian clothes. On the desk were writing materials of all kinds: a leather writing-pad, a fountain pen, various pencils, a scribbling-block, a roller-blotter; but these were all new, as though they had never been used. There were also two telephones and an internal telephone. The room had only one door, the one by which I had come in. He had kept me waiting, therefore, for about half an hour for some special reason, difficult to divine, and not because he was writing or receiving a visitor.

From the desk, my eyes went on to the man himself. I realized for the first time that he had an aquiline nose and slightly swollen cheeks. Strange, for I had never noticed this before; I thought he had a straight nose and flat cheeks. The aquiline nose, with its narrow nostrils and a small, aristocratic prominence in the middle, denoted authority and the will to command; the swollen cheeks, vanity. Suddenly I became aware of something else: when I had entered, he had received me standing up behind the desk but without shaking my hand. "As I was passing through," I said, "I thought I would come and see you. I thought it might give you pleasure to see an old friend again."

He looked at me for a moment in silence with his curious pale, unmoving eyes and finally said : "A pleasure, yes, it is always a pleasure to me to see you. But as for coming to see me here"—and he emphasized the "here" by a pause— "that's another matter. You did right to come if you have something to communicate to me, something to ask me, something to propose; but you did wrong if you came simply to look me up."

The voice was slow, emphatic, weary, as though to bring home to me that he was speaking to me merely out of courtesy. "Why?" I asked.

"Because this is my place of work and I cannot afford the luxury of receiving friends like this, simply to have a little conversation."

"I see, you're very busy."

He started laughing, with a strange laugh, partly polite and partly ironical, which left his eyes completely motionless. "No, I'm not very busy. In fact, for the moment anyhow, I have nothing to do. But it's also true, in a way, that I'm extremely busy."

"I don't understand; are you busy or are you not busy?"

He assumed a reasonable, didactic tone in which I suddenly recognized his best quality of former days—his lucid consciousness of his own manner of acting and his facility in translating it into clear argument. "I *am* busy doing what I was called to this position to do, and I am *not* busy because, as I said, there is not much to do for the moment. But I am busy being what I am, yes, very busy."

"I'm sorry, but I still don't understand you."

He gazed at me for a moment, as though weighing the pros and cons of this conversation. Then he said : "And

171

yet there's nothing obscure in what I'm saying. I have two things to do here: the first is what is called my work; the second, much more important, is the exercise of power."

"The exercise of power? I'm beginning to see . . ."

"It's time you did. Well then, why is the exercise of power so much more important than the work? Because, whereas the work is an ordinary job of a bureaucratic kind which, fundamentally, does not concern me in any way and which might be carried out by anybody, the exercise of power, on the other hand, is something that affects me closely, that concerns me personally and, I am convinced, requires a precise vocation and special gifts to tackle it."

"And you have this vocation and these gifts—isn't that so?"

He looked at me, hesitated and then, once again, led on by his own self-knowledge as if by a mirage, gave way to his own kind of almost ingenuous sincerity: "I did not think I had them. I was convinced, on the contrary, that I was in no way cut out for power. Naturally I knew that power existed, but I wrote it off, judging it from a moralist's point of view, as a thing devoid of real importance. A thing not to be taken into consideration, especially on the part of an intellectual. Then, once I was in this room, seated in this armchair, I discovered in myself gifts and a vocation hitherto unsuspected. And, above all, I understood."

"What did you understand?"

"I discovered that, at a certain level and in certain situations, work no longer counts, is no longer anything more than one aspect—and not even the most important—of the exercise of power. And that this exercise is, on the other hand, in itself, even by itself, even without the accompaniment of a regular, proper job, an occupation, a profession."

He spoke with warmth and smiled at me with a victorious look, like a conjuror demonstrating and explaining the workings of his trick. I said, rather vaguely: "Oh well, power is power, as we know."

"Tautological but exact," he commented with a smile, "certainly power is power. But let us be specific, please. In my case what is power?"

I looked at him in surprise and repeated, like a parrot: "Yes indeed, what is it?"

"Power," he began, in a soft, insinuating, didactic tone of voice, "is, in the first place, this dark suit, this dark tie, this white shirt. D'you remember my old trousers, my wind-jackets? All that is finished."

"Power is in one's clothes? Quite right."

"Certainly: quite right. And then power is this room in which I sit for six hours a day. Please observe the carpet, the hangings on the walls, the frescoes on the ceiling, this desk, my big chair, your small chair: all this is power."

"Clearly," I commented with conviction.

"My time-table is power. My arrival introduces—how shall I say?—a soul into a body that lies inert and apathetic. I am the soul of this part of the building. The soul of the anteroom where sits the usher who showed you in, of the adjoining room where sits my woman secretary. My soul, that is, my power, reaches on one side to the record office and on the other to the far end of the corridor. When I am not here, everything is suspended, is in expectation; when I am here, everything functions. That is power."

He was silent for a moment, and I had almost the impression that I could hear him panting with some kind of excitement. Then he resumed: "Inside this room, power lies in the two telephones which I can use both at the same time, holding one receiver in my hand and clasping the other between my cheek and my shoulder. It is also in this

173

internal telephone by which I can communicate with the usher and with my secretary. It is in this writing-pad, this inkstand, this scribbling-block. It is true that I don't telephone, I don't communicate by the internal telephone, I don't write; but I could."

"Yes," I remarked, "these are, so to speak, the tokens of power, the significant signs. But power as an occupation—in what does that consist?"

He started laughing again, and replied: "Power as an occupation consists in transforming any sort of activity, including work, into manifestations of power."

"Explain."

"Well, for example: I leave this room to go to the bathroom, in order to fulfil a natural need. I go out with my head erect, my chest thrown out, my arms hanging at my sides, my eyes looking straight ahead. The usher, when he sees me, rises to his feet. There, then, is an act of the most ordinary, everyday kind transformed into a manifestation of power."

This time I too started to laugh. "It can't be denied," I said, "that, in spite of power, you've kept your sense of humour."

He laughed too. "Very well," he said, "here's another example, in connection with work. You know what the firm is concerned with, that has its head office in this building. But the real work is entirely done by lower-grade functionaries. As one rises in the scale, the work becomes more and more a pretext, an opportunity for power; and finally, in the highest grades, it evaporates and disappears: nothing is left but power, an end in itself."

"Give me an example."

"Well, I don't know. Let's suppose it has to be decided whether to open an office of ours in a certain foreign city.

Is this office necessary, is it useful, is it functional, is it opportune? I don't know. I only know that the creation of this office allows power to manifest itself."

"And in what way?"

"That's simple: I draw up a report which is exhaustive without taking any definite line, then I have it typed and I ask for an appointment with the Chairman. He receives me, I go in and explain the case, and I ask him to read the report. He reads it, he comments upon it, I reply, we have a long discussion. Now I ask you, which has been more important in this business, power or work? I say power. In fact—does the Chairman decide to create the office? He has exercised power. Does the Chairman decide *not* to create the office? Equally, he has exercised power. Or again: does the Chairman demur, does he say neither yes nor no? For the third time he has exercised power."

He looked at me, shook his head, and smiled in a triumphant, ironical manner. "Yes," I said, "that's right. Nevertheless this firm does not depend entirely on this sort of ritual. There are, there must be practical results as well . . ."

"Of course there are. There are, but in the lower grades, as I said before, just as in the higher grades there is what you call the ritual of power. Take, for example, the meeting which the Board of Directors holds annually in the Board Room on the ground floor. The Board of Directors is in reality composed of distinguished persons who do not direct anything. Yet at the same time they do direct. Just as I myself do not do anything here but at the same time am extremely busy. They direct, because without their names and without their backing the practical results would not be reached. Now I, like you, once thought that a Board of Directors of this kind, purely honorary, served no purpose. But after having been present at the meeting and having

175

listened to the speeches made by some of the members—
speeches, let me emphasize, of an absolutely formal kind—
I changed my mind, or rather, I discovered an immense
territory whose existence I had not previously suspected."

He had become serious now. And I, in turn, asked him
seriously : "And what is this territory?"

Gravely, he replied : "It is, to be precise, the territory of
that magical, enchanted, esoteric fact which is power. The
boundless territory in which actions acquire a significance
very different from the significance they have according to
common sense, precisely because they are performed in the
exercise of power. You spoke of ritual. Well, for once, without intending it, you used the right term. It is indeed a
question of ritual."

At this point I interposed. "There is, however, a difference between you and the Chairman, for instance. You,
so to speak, are acting a part, that is, you are conscious of
the transformation that power introduces into things. But
the Chairman is not. He believes in power, and that's that."

He started laughing, in a slightly unpleasant, even though
friendly, way. "Another error, another piece of naïveté. The
Chairman is by no means unconscious of it, and not only
the Chairman but even my secretary, even the usher. This
is the point : man always knows what he is doing, even
when it may seem that he doesn't know."

I made as though to rise. "I understand," I said. "Then
the only thing for me is to go away. It seems to me that
the little chat with a friend passing through is really impossible in this place of rites and ceremonies."

He rose too, looked at me and then burst into a fit of
amused, almost childish laughter. "All right, go away then,
I won't keep you. But in your case too the transmutation
of values that goes with power has come about—and how !

We've had a little chat, that's true; but this little chat, precisely because you have had it here, and with me, has been changed, as it progressed, into a manifestation of power."

"Of what power?"

"Why, of *mine*, of course!"

# Proto

As soon as I had taken my degree, I felt lost. At the elementary school I had had a master, at the high school a professor, at the university a tutor; and now, all of a sudden, there I was, left to myself, with nobody to teach me, or rather to give me the impression of having the authority of a teacher. Culture, to me, was a religion, not to say a fetish. In this religion there were the officiating priests, that is to say, the professors; there were the esoteric texts, that is, the matters taught; finally there were the faithful, that is, the students; but there was not—and how could there have been?—the act of learning as it is normally understood. This explains the contradiction in me: I had been an extremely bad scholar; but at the same time no one had been more assiduous and (apparently) more attentive. And not unnaturally, for I had sat in the lecture-hall as in a temple, with the same devotion and, let it also be said, with the same almost mystical suspension of the intellectual faculties. I gazed at the professor, I hung upon his lips, but I neither understood nor learned anything.

What about the exams, someone will ask. Well, for the exams I had recourse to memory. However impossible it may seem, that was exactly what I did: for years and years I sat for the exams after learning by heart everything which other students usually remember from having mastered it intellectually. In any case this did not cost me any great effort: I have an exceptional memory. And then, as I

178

answered the professors' questions mechanically and obtusely, I could not help having a feeling of satisfaction: in this way the ritual aspect of culture was confirmed and made to prevail over its other characteristics.

Little, in fact, is needed to transform a piece of historical knowledege, an algebraical formula, a literary quotation, a scientific notion into a magic slogan: all that is necessary is to repeat them like a parrot, without understanding, or trying to understand, their meaning. Of course this was not the best system for passing exams; thus as a student I was frequently ploughed, and the professors, astonished at such stubbornness, would often ask me the obvious question: "Why, what d'you come to school for?" What could I have answered? That what mattered to me was not to learn but to sit in front of somebody who was teaching? I preferred to remain silent.

Having taken a degree in Letters with a thesis which I got a student friend of mine to write for me (for payment; and what did it matter whether I wrote it myself or not? What mattered supremely was that it should be presented, in ritual fashion), I felt, as I have already said, lost. For some time I continued to attend the university and perhaps I might have been on the way to becoming one of those eternal students who go on collecting degrees until they are old, if it had not been that my conception of culture as a ritual prevented me: the degree was a kind of initiation; once it had happened, it could not be repeated. Then I started attending lectures; but here too there was a disadvantage: the lecturers were always different; and what I needed, instead, was a teacher to follow through the years, always the same one. Finally, in despair, I enrolled at a school of languages, choosing, on account of its difficulty which promised me a prolonged course of study, Japanese.

179

But in the meantime I had become lazy; and I no longer felt like writing exercises, or, even less, learning by heart the things I did not understand. I left the school of languages.

What with all these attempts and experiments, I was now past thirty; and my father, who had other sons to be started in professions, was urging me to get to work. But what work? Of teaching there could be no question; my memory had got rid of all the knowledge accumulated during my school and university years, just as a sick stomach banishes heavy food that has been swallowed without chewing. So I told my father that I was ready to accept any sort of employment. It so happened that my father had been a school friend of a so-called "tycoon". He went to see him, explained my case and returned triumphant: there was a job going; I was to present myself next morning, without more ado, at the import-export office of Signor Proto, my future boss.

Talk about presentiments! As I went through the ugly, sordid streets full of old shops, dusty offices and humble but crowded bars of the commercial quarter near the station, I had, all at once, a kind of shudder of premonition, as if I had been a pilgrim and had recognized, with the eye of faith, the privileged seat of my religion. "This is the place," I could not help thinking, "this is the place, I am certain of it, this is the place." I found the nineteenth-century building, dull, gloomy and with peeling plaster, in which Proto had his offices; the staircase, smelly and encrusted with grime, was almost in darkness; then there were two glass doors with the inscription : "J. Proto, Export-Import."

I stopped a moment to get my breath, wondering what that mysterious "J" could mean : Julius? Jesus?; then I pushed open the doors and went in. My heart was beating fast; not because I had run up the stairs four at a time, but because of the confirmation in my mind of the presentiment that I was going to find myself very soon face to face with the man I had been looking for—ever since my distant childhood, it might be said. An elderly usher led me along a corridor and showed me into a large, bright, clean room. There were two desks, facing one another. One of them was unoccupied; behind the other sat Proto.

I looked at him, and immediately I thought: "That's the man, that's really the man, there's no doubt about it: that's him." Proto made a sign to me to sit down. This I did very willingly, for my knees were giving way and I could hardly breathe. I sat down opposite him and, while he was speaking, observed him intently.

The first thing that struck me was the conspicuous, heavy coarseness of his figure. Proto was corpulent in an inert, weighty manner, like a sack full to overflowing. Massive of shoulder, he had a thick neck, short arms, stumpy, shapeless hands. His head was spherical, his hair shorn almost to nothing, the arches of his eyebrows were swollen, his eyes small, his mouth tumid and expressionless. He kept one hand on the desk, with a cigarette held between two fingers: I took a side-look at the palm and trembled with repugnance; it was a conflux of little cushions of red flesh and it seemed astonishing that the fist could be clenched. Proto started to question me about my studies, about my life. He had a deep bass voice, cold and brutal—just the voice I had foreseen he would have.

He was still questioning me when there entered a little dark woman, tiny and elegant, to whom Proto briefly introduced me: "My wife." I watched her bend down towards the big spherical head of her husband while he inclined his

181

fleshy ear towards her thin lips, and she, for a moment, whispered something to him. Then she straightened up again and made a gesture which to me, like Proto's voice, was also foreseeable and in a way foreseen: she took his hand—I should say his paw—and kissed it with fanatical, sensual devotion. Again I thought: "That's the man, that really is the man," and I had a sudden, irresistible feeling of envy: I too should have liked to kiss that big, hairy hand. She turned, looked at me and said unexpectedly: "Excuse me. But you understand certain feelings, don't you?" I bowed slightly without speaking and felt myself blushing.

When his wife had gone out, Proto stretched out his short arm for a bunch of papers that lay on the desk, handed them to me and, indicating the desk opposite his own, said: "Sit down there. From today that's your place." I obeyed joyfully; I had feared that I might be relegated to another room. But, as I was on the point of sitting down, Proto's voice made me jump: "Could you do me a favour?" I twisted round towards him, and he explained: "I have a stiff leg, I move with difficulty and I can't stoop; this, incidentally, is the reason for my corpulence. Would you mind tying up this shoe for me?" I scarcely allowed him to finish; I knelt down in front of the foot he was holding out to me. He held it well up and I placed my two hands on the lace that had come undone; then, bending down a little, I touched the toe of his shoe lightly with my lips. I tied a good double knot and rose to my feet, looking up at Proto as I did so. Had he noticed that I had kissed his foot? His face was impassive; truly it had some quality of a fetish or a statue. "Thank you so much," he said; and I went back and sat down at my desk.

Since that day everything in my life has changed. To

182

outward appearance I have settled down, with a job, an office, a time-table, a superior; in reality I have found the spiritual guide I was seeking. Someone may well ask me what kind of a spiritual guide can he be, this Proto who is so gross, so uncouth and, above all, so expressionless. And I reply that he is a spiritual guide precisely because there is no reason why he should be. Indeed, precisely because it is too absurd to imagine that Proto is a teacher, precisely for that reason I am certain that he is.

Two years have now gone by and I am still sitting in the same place in Proto's office, opposite him. Every now and then I raise my eyes, look at him and wait for him to look back at me, lift his hand, open his mouth and, in a few or many words, reveal his message to me. But I am in no hurry; the revelation may come in five, or ten, or twenty years; what matters most is not that it should come but that I should be sure that it may come. At any moment, or even never.

# Smells and the Bone

The world, it is certain, is made up of bones and smells. It is made up of bones when, for some mysterious reason that I cannot explain, I am stronger than the world; it is made up of smells when, for other and no less mysterious reasons, the world is stronger than me. In the first case, a drastic reduction takes place: the world becomes nothing but a bone; in the second, a stupefying explosion: the world is a million, a million million smells. The reduction of the world to a bone is accompanied by somewhat disagreeable feelings and manifestations: my coat bristles, I grind my teeth, I bark, I foam at the mouth, I fall upon it, I bite; the explosion of smells is also accompanied by special behaviour: nose to the ground, I pursue, one after the other, the infinite number of smells that go to compose reality; or else, sitting on my hind legs, head raised and nostrils opened wide, I interpret with voluptuous pleasure the innumerable olfactory messages that reach me from every direction.

The variety of smells is infinite. There are four-legged smells, that is, cats, dogs, horses; two-legged, that is, human beings; smells that crawl, that is, snakes; that fly, that is, birds; that swim, that is, fish; that swarm, that is, bees, ants and insects in general. There are green smells, grass for instance; blue ones, the sky; yellow ones, the sun; red ones, blood. The smells that move fast are called aeroplanes, motor-cars, bicycles, lizards, hares; the smells that make a noise, radio, television, gramophones, bells, hornets; the smells that stay quiet, generally the pieces of furniture in the house, when there is no one there and the rooms are in the dark.

Of course there are good smells and bad smells. Without troubling to draw up an impossible catalogue, I will say merely that the good smells are those which most resemble the smell of putrefaction and the bad ones those which resemble it less. It must not be supposed, however, that there is any arbitrary scale of values. In reality, putrefaction is synonymous with personality; and this is because length of time is indispensable for the development of personality, that is, of putrefaction. The fact of the matter is that it is impossible to achieve a certain degree of putrefaction—that is, it is impossible to acquire a personality recognizable as such—all in a moment: time is needed. Children, in fact, and new objects have no smell, that is, no personality; whereas an old man, or a carpet impregnated with the dust of a century, exhale numerous and subtly blended smells, that is, they have complicated, profound personalities.

Another smell that has an irresistible effect upon us dogs, rather like the effect of a drug upon an addict, is the smell of our master. This is a case of an indefinable, so to speak metaphysical, smell. It lies at the root of the faithfulness for which we are famed: a dog will descend to any depth of meanness in order to follow perpetually the traces of this smell. Incidentally, I should like it to be noted that dogs' masters invariably have what may be termed the "master" smell. It is strange, it is incomprehensible, but it is so.

Furthermore, with regard to the reduction of the world to a bone, that is, to the transmutation of infinite and infinitely blended smells into a single, brutal, simple bone, this comes about whenever a dog gets the impression that the smell is about to be withdrawn from him. The sniffing

185

of smells on the part of dogs closely resembles the act of contemplation in human beings: the dog loses himself in the smell, forgets himself, is nullified. But if it happens that someone tries to remove the smell from him, then the dog becomes a dog again and the world becomes a bone.

Let me give an example. A stocking belonging to my young mistress is lying on the floor; I go up to it, I sniff it, I dissolve into a million smells, each more delicious than the last; but all of a sudden the servant-girl's hand passes in front of my nose in order to pick up the stocking. Then there is no longer any smell, there is no longer anything, the world has become a bone, and I am the dog to whom the bone belongs and who will defend it at all costs, ready to fall upon it, to bite, to tear it to pieces.

It may be that all this will seem to you rather too philosophical. But when you know the place in which I find myself at present, you will understand the reason for this philosophy. It is the philosophy of despair. In short, I have been shut up for two days in a cage at the municipal kennels, under observation, to see whether by any chance I am suffering from rabies. Rabies, in case you do not know, is merely the state of mind—raging mad, indeed—into which a dog falls when, for some private reason of his own, he becomes firmly and finally convinced that there are no smells, that there have never been any smells, and that the world is a bone, nothing but an enormous, massive, dull, shapeless, frightful bone. And as to why I am here, that is a story I should like to tell you.

I must go back to my relationship with my young mistress. I was her dog; she was my mistress. By this I mean that, as well as being composed of an infinite number of smells, all of them delicious, my young mistress had, in a most conspicuous degree, the smell which is powerful above

186

all others, the "master" smell. Of course my mistress's father and mother and sister also had this "master" smell about them; but my young mistress was, so to speak, more my mistress than the others. I will not stop to describe in detail my relationship with this extremely charming girl; I should have to enumerate, one by one, the infinite fragrances that emanated, violent and inexhaustible, from her person, beginning from the tips of her toes and upwards to her hair. I only wish to note a singular phenomenon: the perception of her personal smells opened up the world for me, so to speak, that is, it revealed to me, as though by sympathy, the endless variety of smells which are commonly designated by the name of reality. I would, for instance, be following my mistress on a walk in the park—a walk, incidentally, that she was taking for my sake, so that I might stretch my legs and fulfil the needs of nature; and then— a miracle indeed!—just as though the boundary between *her* smells and those of the outside world had been suddenly removed, I would feel that my nostrils had penetrated, so to speak, from the perception of the Particular to the perception—the ineffable perception—of the All.

Yes indeed, I identified myself to such a degree with my mistress's smells that I no longer existed; and thus it was perfectly easy for me to go over from this initial smell to the smell, let us say, of the sun which warms and illuminates all. But I am aware that I am not able to explain myself very well. Suffice it to say, therefore, that the love that human beings talk about so much is no more than a coarse caricature of the feeling which a dog can experience when walking behind his mistress, in a park on a fine sunny day.

And then, suddenly, my young mistress became engaged to a young man called Piero, a lawyer by profession, extremely clean, however, and therefore almost devoid of personality. In becoming engaged she forgot her dog, she forgot, that is, that for her dog she was the sole means of communication with the world; and her fiancé, odiously clean as I have already said, stuck closely to her. From the day of her engagement my young mistress never again belonged only, and entirely, to me: her fiancé came with us on our walks, he was in the car, he was at table, he was in the shops, he was there in his own home (but here they shut me out on the terrace and left me there for hours), he was in the country, he was at the seaside, he was everywhere. Someone may object: why not become fond of this fiancé? In any case he had no smells, or hardly any; and besides, he lacked the most important smell, I mean the "master" smell.

After that, at first almost imperceptibly, then with increasing rapidity, the world for me lost all its smells, one after the other; it became transformed, in the end, into a single, unendurable bone. There had been a million smells, all of them evanescent, exquisitely blended, rich in subtle gradations; the bone was one single thing, dull, shapeless, enormous, ferocious. To make a comparison, the smells had been like music full of infinite harmonies; but the bone was merely a single, sombre, truculent thump on a drum. Similarly, I had passed from the true ecstasy of sniffing to the rage inspired by the bone. Indeed the entire world was a bone; they wanted to snatch it away from me; I had to defend it at all costs. Strange to say, this rage was calm and devoid of external manifestations. I was raging mad, but no one was aware of it.

The wedding-day arrived and the house was invaded by guests, all of them bones, nothing but bones, no smells at all. I wandered round amongst all those legs without even trying to sniff them; anyhow I would not have been able to smell anything, so bursting with fury was I. Someone stooped down to stroke me, someone else gave me a kick: it was all the same to me. Actually I was in process of charging myself with rage, like a steam engine under pressure; I did not see, or smell, or perceive anything; I was merely agitated by an increasing fury because the whole world, by now, was for me a bone and I was afraid of losing this bone, and so I felt a sort of urge at the corners of my mouth and in the hinge of my jaw and several times it was only with difficulty that I restrained myself from attacking and biting.

Attacking and biting whom? I do not know, somebody or something that wanted at that moment to steal the world from me—that is, the enormous, disproportionate bone that the world had become to me. But, at the same time, I felt that until yesterday evening the world, for me, had been my young mistress, she and nothing else, she who with her infinite smells had prepared me for the perception of the entire universe; and I became obscurely conscious that the stealer of the bone was the bridegroom. All of a sudden this suspicion became certainty; I saw red and, overflowing with hatred, set out in search of my enemy.

Perhaps it would be a good thing, at this point, to give a description of myself. I am a brindled boxer, tawny with dark streaks, the hinder part of my body slim and elegant, the forepart massive. I have a black muzzle, like that of a Chinese dragon; deep winding furrows on my head and round my mouth give me an almost sad expression; but at the same time the bull neck, the conformation of the mouth with the lower teeth covering the upper teeth, and the fixed, red eye, all go to make up a terrifying physiognomy. I am a fighting dog; if I bite I do not abandon my prey, I am relentless, I pull, I rend, I tear asunder . . . And so, here I was in search of my mistress's fiancé. My search did not last long. In a small secluded room I found the two of them, she standing in front of a looking-glass; and he behind her, busy adjusting the zip fastener on the back of her dress.

I did not bark, I did not howl, I did not make a sound. Suddenly, with an irresistible rush, I leapt upon him. Instinctively I aimed at his neck : he, also instinctively, lifted his arm to his face to defend himself; I bit him in the arm, deeply, and for some seconds I remained hanging there, my teeth fastened in blood and flesh. Then, at her cries, people came rushing in; they seized me, tore me away, carried me off . . .

And now here I am, in a cage at the municipal kennels, under observation. I know what awaits me : either the world, for me, becomes free and manifold and open, becomes once more the world of smells, and then I shall return home; or else it continues to be a bone, nothing but a bone which I, in my rage, am afraid of losing, and then, after a few days, I shall be put into the gas chamber. The alternative does not escape me; yet at the same time I cannot, for all my efforts, succeed in perceiving any kind of smell. Yes, the world is a bone; and I have fixed my teeth in it and I will die rather than let go.